SALTED CARAMEL
DREAMS

CURL UP WITH ALL OF THE SWIRL NOVELS!

Pumpkin Spice Secrets by Hillary Homzie
Peppermint Cocoa Crushes by Laney Nielson
Cinnamon Bun Besties by Stacia Deutsch
Salted Caramel Dreams by Jackie Nastri Bardenwerper

SALTED CARAMEL
DREAMS

Jackie Nastri
Bardenwerper

SKY PONY PRESS

Sky Pony Press
New York

To Ceci and Bo—may you always follow your dreams.

First Edition

This is a work of fiction. Names, characters, places, and incidents are from the author's imagination and used fictitiously.

Sky Pony Press books may be purchased in bulk at special discounts for sales promotion, corporate gifts, fund-raising, or educational purposes. Special editions can also be created to specifications. For details, contact the Special Sales Department, Sky Pony Press, 307 West 36th Street, 11th Floor, New York, NY 10018 or info@skyhorsepublishing.com.

Sky Pony® is a registered trademark of Skyhorse Publishing, Inc.®, a Delaware corporation.

www.skyponypress.com

10 9 8 7 6 5 4 3 2 1

Library of Congress Cataloging-in-Publication Data is available on file.

Cover design by Liz Casal
Cover photo credit: iStock Photo

Paperback ISBN: 978-1-5107-3010-6
Ebook ISBN: 978-1-5107-3014-4

Printed in Canada

Chapter One
THE SECRET

The fall air, cool and breezy with a tinge of winter bite, tickles my skin as Kiara and I burst out of Dolce. Stomachs heaving and hands wrapped around our warm drinks, we try to steady ourselves as we navigate Southfield's infamous sidewalks, cracked and broken from the roots of the now red and yellow maple trees above. But between all our laughter and those stupid platform shoes we're both wearing, it isn't easy. First Kiara's ankle goes, then mine.

"Watch those drinks!" Kiara says. "Don't let them spill!"

"I won't," I say. "Who needs ankles when you've got salted caramel steamers?"

"Not me," says Kiara, eyes twinkling in the afternoon sun. "I'd take salted caramel any day."

We hold on to each other as we leap over another crack, joking the whole time. It's been a long day of school—seventh-grade days feel so much longer than sixth, with all their worksheets and lecturing and writing—and it feels good to be out in the cool air, listening to Kiara tell her stories. The sun is shining, my homework load is light, and we're almost at DIY Club, my favorite place to be. What could be better? I breathe in deep, savoring the wafting smell of our sweet drinks as we reach the crosswalk on Main Street.

"So, ready to finish your bag today?" I ask, envisioning our almost-completed DIY projects. "I'm thinking mine could be a good addition to JKDesigns."

"Oh yeah, definitely," she says.

Whenever we're not talking about school or DIY club or her crush Carter, we're often discussing JKDesigns, the Etsy shop we're planning to launch during winter break. Just mentioning the shop usually gets us talking for hours about our dream of becoming big fashion design stars, famous before we turn thirteen. But today when I mention it, Kiara looks tired.

"Hey, everything okay?" I ask.

"Yeah, sure," she says. "It's just . . ."

She pauses as the crossing guard, Mike, holds out his hand, stopping us at the corner. Usually Kiara likes to tease him about one of the million sports teams he's obsessed with, but today she remains quiet. Worried, I shoot him a smile, hoping he knows we're not mad at him. He smiles back as we walk across.

Once we reach the other side, Kiara starts again. "So, well, you know, there is this one thing I've been meaning to tell you. I was actually gonna wait until tomorrow, but since you're talking about JKDesigns and this is our last fall DIY class, I probably should let you know . . ."

"What?" I ask, taking a sip of my drink. It's not like Kiara to keep secrets. Especially about something big. "What's going on?"

Kiara, cheeks still flushed from laughing, bites down on her lip.

"Well . . . It's just that I'm not sure I'm gonna do DIY club this winter," she says. "I was thinking of trying out for basketball instead."

I force myself to swallow.

"Basketball . . . Really? Whoa. That's cool," I say, trying to sound natural. Like my best friend hasn't just dropped a bomb of a secret she's been withholding for who-knows-how-long.

Kiara looks away, letting her long brown hair dance across her freckled face. She's gripping her salted caramel steamer tight, and I wonder if she remembers the day we created the drink last summer after trying every flavor combination in the shop. Steamed milk, caramel sauce, dark salted chocolate syrup, and a sprinkling of coconut, all blended together. The coconut had been Kiara's finishing touch. I'm still convinced it was that final flourish that made the drink worthy of a place on the permanent menu, though Kiara insists it has more to do with how often we order it. Either way, I've always been proud to see our drink etched out in pink chalk.

I wonder how often we'll be ordering them if Kiara makes the team. How much time does basketball take?

Kiara turns to me and smiles, looking at me for the first time since breaking her news. "Mom says I should get involved in something new, and I *have* always liked shooting hoops with my brother. So I thought basketball might be fun. Especially since rumor has it you-know-who is trying out for the boys' team," she says with a wink.

Of course. Carter. I should've known that boy would be behind this. Not that I can blame her—Kiara isn't the only girl obsessed with his mischievous smile—though besides that grin he's always seemed a little average to me. I'd like to think a guy worth crushing on would have something to him that was just, well, a little more special.

But I'm also the girl who hasn't had a crush since Connor O'Neil in fourth grade. Back then, he had this awesome mop of blond hair and was learning how to play the guitar and used to turn around and stare at me like I was someone he wanted to get to know. I was too shy to talk to him, but after a while I started to like him. But then as soon as I did, he ratted out me and Kiara for passing notes. Guess that's what all the staring was about. After that, I pretty much swore off boys. Meaning, I'm not exactly one to offer advice on the topic.

So even though I worry that Carter is a bit boring for someone as fun and talented as my best friend, what can I do but hope he likes Kiara back? Maybe basketball will be just her ticket. That is, if Kiara makes the team. Which shouldn't be too hard, seeing as ever since we turned twelve she's shot up like a beanpole, leaving me a good six inches behind.

"Hey, you know, you should try out too, Jas," Kiara says, interrupting my thoughts.

But I just shake my head. "Thanks, but I don't think basketball's for me."

"Yeah, I get it," she says, not even trying to change my mind.

Though really, it'd be weird if she did. Measuring in at five feet, I seem to have inherited my height from the Colombian side of the family—none of the women in Mom's family are taller than five-foot-three. So even if I were interested, it would be pretty tough for me to make the team.

And that's probably for the better. I've got enough going on already with DIY club. Taught by Ms. Chloe, one of Mom's Pinterest-obsessed friends who designs and sells clothing, it's a class for kids interested in all things design. We've created beaded necklaces and earrings, hair accessories, and more. My favorite classes are the ones related to fashion design. In the past couple years, I've gone from not knowing how to thread a needle to designing my own bags, and I hope to move on to clothing soon. I love the whole process—the design sketching, then the fabric selection, the sewing, and the finish work. Each time I create something new I feel like I've climbed a mountain. Which is why I can't wait to launch JKDesigns with Kiara. I'm hoping that through our Etsy shop, I'll be able to build a portfolio that will one day get me into a fashion design program for college.

I smile, envisioning the products we've already decided on for the shop. Kiara's going to have a section with these cool wire hair accessories she's great at making, and I'm going to sew a line of Jasmine-original tote bags that will have lots of inside pockets and this cool outside stitching in contrasting colors. I'm hoping they'll be popular, given that Southfield is a beach town, right on the beautiful Connecticut coast. Yet my real dream is to one day sell custom clothes, just as soon as I can perfect my skills at turning my sketches into actual sewing patterns. So far I haven't been able to design anything requiring an actual waistline, but every night I spend at least an hour trying. Hopefully, soon I'll get one right and be selling my own designs.

I take another sip of salted caramel steamer and think of the bag waiting for me in the second-story studio above Hank's Dry Cleaning. All day I've been thinking about the little iridescent beads I'm going to stitch onto the perimeter of the top flap. Ms. Chloe spent the entire last class teaching me the technique, and I've been practicing at home all week. Last night I even stitched an entire row of beads without stopping. This was the news I was going to share with Kiara before she brought up the basketball thing.

"Maybe you'll have time for DIY club *and* basketball," I say, my mood rebounding as I think of the beads. "Or at least meet a lot more customers for JKDesigns!"

"Yeah, I don't know if I'll make the classes, but I'll definitely be talking up JKDesigns," Kiara says.

I nod, relieved. Maybe basketball will turn out to be a good thing. An opportunity to spread the news about our shop.

"When are the tryouts, anyway?" I ask.

"They start tomorrow. For three days. So I guess I'll know by the end of the week."

"Wow. That's fast."

"I know," she says.

We walk the rest of the stairs in silence. I focus on the climb until I can smell the cinnamon and clove oils Ms. Chloe burns to "help the creative juices flow." I breathe them in through my nose, hoping the scents will relax me. Miraculously, it works. By the time we reach the bright orange and teal walls of the studio, I'm ready to sew.

"Good afternoon, ladies," Ms. Chloe says as we enter.

"Good afternoon, Ms. Chloe," we say. We walk by a table of sixth graders before claiming our usual spot in the back.

"All right, now that you're all here, is everyone ready to finish those bags today?" she asks.

"Definitely," says Kiara, shedding her coat. "Though I think I may need a little help using the machine. I kind of messed up last time."

Kiara holds up her bag, pointing out the imperfections. She's never been big into sewing, and I can tell she's antsy to finish.

"Of course!" says Ms. Chloe. She whisks Kiara off to one of the sewing machines, pausing just long enough to flick on the radio as she passes by.

And then for the next hour everything is perfect. With the music flowing, I relax, letting myself sing along to the Top 40 as my stitches become tighter, the beads even straighter than I was able to get last night. *I can't wait to use this at school*, I think, happy to have an excuse to retire my practical, yet very boring, purple backpack I've had since I was ten. The bag I'm making today isn't a tote, but a messenger bag, and a perfect copy of one I saw online for hundreds of dollars—but with my own spin on the decoration. I'm hoping someday I'll be able to sell one like it on our shop site.

"This is looking phenomenal," Ms. Chloe says, surprising me from behind. "You're a real natural at this, Jasmine. Truly, you have such an eye."

I look down and smile. "Thanks, Ms. Chloe."

"No, thank *you*. I can't wait to buy one of your Jasmine originals," she says with a wink.

By the time class ends, I'm just a few touches away from finishing and wish I could stay another hour. But dinner at home is always at six, so lingering isn't an option. I grab my coat and give Kiara's hand a quick squeeze as we head toward the staircase.

"Well, that was fun," Kiara says as we reach the street. "I just can't believe today might've been my last class."

"Wow. That's right," I say, and for a second I start to worry all over again.

But Kiara snaps me out of it. "By the way," she says, "I totally forgot to ask you about your latest pattern. Any update?"

I smile as I picture the pinned-together fabric scraps I've assembled on the dress form—really just a secondhand mannequin Mom found for me in a thrift store—in my closet.

"Not much new," I say as we cross Main Street and begin the short walk to our neighborhood. "Still working on it."

"I'm sure you'll get it soon," she says.

"We'll see," I say. "It can't end up worse than the micro dresses."

We erupt into laughter as we think of the matching sundresses I tried to make last summer. They were supposed to have short sleeves and fall to our knees, and I got this pretty Hawaiian print fabric for them. But after pinning the fabric and taking measurements and creating a pattern, I forgot to cut extra fabric for seams. So the sleeves came out too narrow for us to fit our arms in. And the skirt length was way too short—the dresses barely hit our thighs! Talk about a disaster. The only thing I'd been able to save was a little of the fabric, which I used on one of my bags as trim.

"On second thought, maybe you should just stick with the bags," says Kiara.

"Seriously. The patterns sure are easier," I say.

And then before I can think about it anymore, we're at the top of the hill. The spot where we always part ways.

Kiara extends her hand, breaking me away from my thoughts.

"Tick tock, tick tock . . . " she begins.

"Who's the coolest on the block?" I say, slapping her hand with mine. Then we entwine our fingers and laugh before completing the secret handshake we've been perfecting since the fourth grade.

"Well, I'll see you tomorrow, girl," Kiara says with a smile.

"I'll be here, ready to go at seven," I say.

"Can't wait! And don't forget. Friday—sleepover at my place. No matter what," Kiara says, turning back toward her street.

After a quick wave, I do the same. Picking up my pace, I zip my coat a little higher, trying to keep out the cold. The evening air is sharper than it was just last week, a sign of the changing season. I think of Kiara's last words: *Friday. Sleepover. No matter what.* Their warmth hugs me tight as my cheery yellow house comes into focus. I turn into the driveway and breathe in deep, preparing for the chaos that comes with having two parents, twin brothers, and a live-in grandma. Yet as I reach for the doorknob, I find my mind's still filled with doubt. Because as great as this basketball thing may turn out to be for Kiara, I can't quite shake the feeling that everything is about to change.

Chapter Two
INVITATION ONLY

"So wait, what happened again?" I ask, trying to decipher Kiara's words through her laughter.

Kiara's been giggling nonstop ever since I walked over with my sleeping bag to congratulate her on making the team. We're supposed to be watching a movie, one of our favorite Friday night sleepover activities, but every time we go to start it, Kiara thinks of another story from tryouts. I smile as she sits up and tries to slow her breathing enough to talk, grateful she's taking the time to fill me in on all I've missed.

"I told you . . . it was Mary Beth. You know, from homeroom last year? Anyway, she forgot her ankle brace yesterday and she has a really weak ankle, so me and Aliyah snuck into the wood shop for her and took some duct tape to wrap her ankle so it wouldn't twist. And it worked! Last year, she got cut on the second day of tryouts, but this time she made it through. So we decided the tape must've been lucky and that she needed to wear it on the third day too. But then after practice when we were helping her take it off, Beatrice came in and was like, 'you look radioactive in that thing—I bet you could pick up radio stations!' And we all started laughing. But Mary Beth just shrugged and told her she was going to wrap her ankle in tape again today. And she did! Only this time she brought a little radio to clip onto her sneaker. And, get this, she actually did pick up a few stations! It was ridiculous. You should've seen the look on Coach's face when Mary Beth started playing music during suicides . . ."

"Wow, that's crazy," I say, as Kiara keeps laughing and singing the chorus of some song she played for me earlier. Beatrice's favorite, she said. I guess it was on repeat during tryouts. I try to laugh too, but somehow, no matter how many stories Kiara tells me, I just can't seem to. And it's not that the stories aren't funny. It's just that they're different. Mary

Beth, Beatrice, Aliyah. These are girls I only know by name, and up until a few days ago, Kiara didn't know them either. But it seems like the perils of tryouts have drawn them together.

"Yeah, Mary Beth is hilarious," Kiara says. "And Aliyah is just so cool. I wish you could've seen what she was wearing today at practice. She had on these adorable purple and black shorts and these bright green sneakers with, like, glitter sewn into the fabric. You would've loved them. She's actually taking me and Mary Beth to the mall tomorrow so we can get some cool workout clothes of our own."

"Oh. Wow." Her words take the wind right out of me. Going to the mall has always been our thing. And my only plans for tomorrow are walking home from Kiara's house. Not that I tell this to Kiara. Instead I just smile back at her wide grin. "Sounds fun," I say.

"I know, right? I can't wait. Right now I have exactly two pairs of shorts and three tank tops. But now that I made the team, my mom says I can get some new stuff."

"That's really great. She must be so excited," I say, thinking of the smile I received when her mom opened the door.

"Yeah, she's thrilled. I think that's why she's letting us have sundaes for dessert."

"That's right, we should go make some. The ice cream will go great with those cookies my mom made for us," I say, already dreaming of the dulce de leche cookies Mom baked for us this afternoon.

My mom and Kiara's mom met back when they first started working at this marketing agency after college, and then grew even closer after having us and moving to the same neighborhood. So as soon as Mom learned Kiara made the team, she booked it to the kitchen and got to work making Kiara's favorite cookies, even though she was supposed to be working from home.

"Oh, those cookies. They're the best!" Kiara says, standing. "And now we can make cookie sundaes! With different sauces! I think we have chocolate and strawberry."

"Any salted caramel?" I ask.

Kiara laughs. "I wish. Though we can always sneak out to Dolce . . ."

"Right. Not like your parents would freak out or anything."

"True. And I don't want anything keeping me from

basketball!" Kiara smiles wide. "Which reminds me, I almost forgot. Carter today, oh-em-gee. You should've seen him—we shared the court with the guys for the last ten minutes of practice, and he was on fire! Hit every shot he took."

"Whoa, sounds like he's really good. You talk to him at all?"

Kiara shakes her head. "Not today, but we did a little on Thursday. Turns out he and Aliyah live in the same neighborhood. She's gonna give me the inside scoop tomorrow."

"Oh that's awesome," I say. "I'm so glad tryouts went well. Though I did miss you this week. It was so quiet."

Kiara nods as she shuffles over to the freezer. "Aw, believe me, part of me would've much rather been with you. What'd you do at Ms. Chloe's? You finish your bag?"

I smile, excited to have a chance to talk about my week. "Almost. I mean, I probably should stop messing with it, but every time I think it's done, I see a loose thread or get this idea to add more beads. Anyway, it'll soon be done for real."

"That's great," she says.

"I know. I can't wait to use it. Though I'm really

loving this other bag I'm working on too. It's got a ribbon trim and this chain of tassels and pompoms I made. I can see it being a big seller."

"Sounds like it," says Kiara, scooting in. "You have pictures?"

I grab my phone and pull up a picture of the tote.

"Whoa, that's gorgeous! I think I might need one myself."

"Sold," I say, laughing. "My first order!"

"The first of many," Kiara says.

"Definitely. I really am getting excited," I say. "My mom got me this biography of Coco Chanel and it's really motivating me."

Kiara laughs. "Isn't that like your fifth one?"

"What? No!" I say. "The last one was Diane von Furstenberg. The one before that was about Alexander McQueen!"

"Same difference."

I roll my eyes. Kiara's never been a big reader.

"Anyway, I thought we could dabble in a little styling tonight ourselves," Kiara says.

I raise my brow. "I didn't bring any of my sewing things."

"Good, because I wasn't thinking about sewing,

but hair! My mom got this new straightening iron, and I really wanna try it out," Kiara says, digging into her ice cream.

"Oh no, not that again," I say.

"No, this time will be different," Kiara says. "I saw her use it before work the other day and it looks way easier. And her hair looked so silky smooth. Actually, hang on a sec, let me go grab it." Kiara jumps off her stool and heads toward the family room. "Mom, you in there? Hey, I was wondering if we can borrow your hair straightener. Jasmine and I want to try it out ourselves . . ."

Kiara returns a minute later, her steps so quiet I don't hear her until she's almost back at her stool. No matter how many times I sleep over, I can never get over how quiet and peaceful and orderly everything is here. Kiara's house is the polar opposite of mine, which is probably why we spend most of our sleepovers watching movies in the Murphys' basement. Not that there's anything wrong with my house, it's just that at home things are busy. With Kiara's brother away at college, it's just her and her parents. But at my house, there's Mom and Dad and Edwin and Michael and Abuela, who moved in with us last year after she got diabetes. Meaning that no matter the time, there is always someone watching TV or cooking or shouting about something. Sometimes I wonder if that's why I'm so quiet. In a house full of people, conflicts can often drop down out of nowhere like a tornado. Sometimes keeping your mouth shut is the best way to stay safe.

"So you ready?" Kiara asks.

"I guess," I say, savoring the peace. "Though I still doubt it'll get hot enough to tame my hair."

Kiara giggles. "I'm telling you it will. Promise."

Visions of my black curls frizzed out like a bird's nest come back to me, and I laugh right along with her, happy to be reliving one of our own private stories. I do Kiara's hair first—it takes less than ten minutes, as her fine brown locks have very little wave to flatten—and then we start on mine. After a few yelps and finger burns, Kiara finishes. When she puts down the straightener, I can still feel some frizz, but the strands I can see seem pretty straight.

"So, what do you think?" she asks, handing me a mirror.

One look and my mouth falls. "Honestly?" I say, holding it up.

"Honestly."

"I think I look like a wet cat!" I say, bursting into laughter. "Look at me!"

The flat hair has thrown my whole face out of balance, accentuating my broad nose and wide eyes, the pimples I can never get rid of on my forehead.

"Seriously? After all my hard work?"

"Sorry, but I don't see being a hair stylist in your future."

"Fair enough," she says, between laughs.

And then with the hair straightener still hot, Kiara throws on her pajamas while I reach for the air mattress we keep blown up underneath Kiara's bed. A minute later, we're both tucked in tight.

"Tick tock, tick tock . . ." Kiara says from under the covers.

"Who's the coolest on the block?" I finish, reaching up to meet her hands.

"Night Jas," she says.

"Night girl," I say.

And then I close my eyes and begin to drift off in Kiara's warm, quiet house. But before sleep can find me, I remember what Kiara said about shopping tomorrow with Aliyah and Mary Beth. And how this time, she didn't even try to invite me.

Chapter Three

THREE'S A CROWD

"So what do you think of the new headbands? Cool, right?" asks Kiara as we walk home from school. It's been a month since she made the team, and today is the first Friday in three weeks that Kiara doesn't have practice. While we always talk during lunch and science class, and have managed to keep up with our nighttime text sessions, walking home from school has been lonely. And as nice as the younger girls are at Ms. Chloe's, they just aren't as good at telling stories and making me laugh as Kiara. So right now, it feels good to have her by my side.

"Yeah, I like them," I say. "Especially that pink one

you showed me. But I still think your wire clips are the coolest. They're just so unique."

"True, but these bands, they seriously may be the way to go. They take like ten minutes to make and girls can wear them all the time. The clips are more like for special occasions, you know?"

"It'll be cool to see what sells best."

"Well, I already have three orders for the bands. I would have four but I gave one to Beatrice for free."

I nod and pull my jacket around me. Three orders. Already. For fancy elastic bands covered with a thin ribbon of polka dots. They're not different or exciting or anything except ordinary. I sigh, wondering how long it'll be before I can even make that many tote bags.

"So you still coming to the game tomorrow?" she asks as we reach the intersection of our roads.

I nod. "Yup. I'll be there."

"You're the best," she says, then grabs my hand, her voice a whisper even though the street's deserted. "Now before I go, I need to fill you in on Carter."

"Yeah, that's right. What's up?"

"He told Aliyah he needs a new lab partner during carpool yesterday," she says. "Turns out Teddy's bombed the past three tests and is moving down a level. So Carter needs to find someone new."

"But everyone's already paired up. What are they gonna do? Make a group of three?"

Kiara brushes the hair off her shoulder and scoots in even closer. "I'm thinking we should volunteer."

"To add Carter?"

"Yeah. Aliyah said he was asking who else in the class is cool, since he only really knew Teddy."

"And lemme guess. She might've mentioned you."

Kiara smirks.

"Wow. This is big news," I say. "Though having him as a lab partner? Don't you think that could be a little too close?"

Kiara shrugs. "Enemies close and crushes closer?"

I force a laugh as she leans in for our handshake.

"Anyway, I'm sure it'll work itself out," she says. "Have a good one, and I'll see you tomorrow!" She shoots me one final wave as she disappears down the street.

At home, I retreat to my room, eager to finish the beadwork on my bag. Yet every time I try to concentrate on my beading, my mind wanders back to Carter and science. Frustrated, I throw down my bag and reach for my backpack instead. For the next two hours I lose myself in the world of homework. I finish up just as I hear the front door slam.

"Pizza's here," Dad says.

Raising my brow, I run toward the door. "Pizza? On a Friday?" Treat night is usually Saturday. Every other night Mom cooks.

"Yeah, surprise," says Mom. "Abuela's doctor's appointment ran late, and then I had to send out that big proposal and pick up the boys, so I thought treat night could come early this week."

I nod as Michael snickers behind me.

"What's that?" I say.

"Shh, you be quiet, Michael Aaron," says Mom, using her you-better-not-mess-with-me voice.

Just hearing her tone gets Edwin laughing. "Yeah, you cut it out Michael Aaron."

"Um, guys, what's going on?" I ask.

"Mom wasn't too busy," says Michael.

"Yeah, she was gonna make chicken and rice. But she spilled it all over the floor!" says Edwin.

The boys erupt into laughter.

I roll my eyes at their laughter, then smile back at Mom.

"Well, pizza sounds great," I say.

Mom sighs, then gives my back a pat. Her hands feel cold and her eyes look tired, which they do a lot now that she has to juggle Abuela's appointments with her work schedule and all the boys' practices. I try to make things easier for her by not asking for rides or homework help, but even so, she often looks overwhelmed.

"Thank you," she says, shuffling back to the kitchen. "Now would you mind calling your grandmother for dinner?"

"Sure," I say, happy to help. I run out of the kitchen and down the steps to the basement room Dad spruced up for Abuela.

I find her hunched over her laptop, video chatting with her sister in Colombia.

"Abuela, dinner's ready," I say.

She looks up and smiles. "Gracias Jasmine, give me five more minutes."

"All right," I say, trying not to laugh. Abuela's about as good at following directions as the twins. "Should I tell Mom to wait?"

She mutes the computer, then lowers her voice. "Depends. What'd she make?"

Again, I fight laughter. I think Mom's a great cook, but Abuela is picky.

"Actually, Dad picked up pizza," I say.

"Oh. Then on second thought, I'll be right up," she says, unmuting the computer. "Jasmine, say hello to your aunt. I need to go freshen."

I do my best to keep up with my great aunt's rapid Spanish before Abuela returns to say goodbye.

"I'll call later," she says, waving to the screen before closing the computer.

Upstairs, we find everyone already seated around the table, the pizza displayed on Mom's favorite serving plates next to a big green salad she made herself.

"This looks great!" I say, eyeing my favorite yellow peppers in the salad.

Mom smiles, then says a quick prayer before letting us dig in.

After dinner, I retreat back to my room, ready to give my beadwork another try. But my hands are still too shaky to get it right. So I cast my bag aside, turn up the radio, and pull out my sketchpad instead. Within minutes, I'm in the zone, the day's troubles forgotten. I work on two new dress designs along with one more bag before deciding it's time for bed.

And by morning I'm feeling more optimistic, the sketching having done its job. *Who cares about headbands when I have a whole fashion career ahead of me*, I think as I throw on my favorite jeans—the ones I distressed myself last year in Spanish class—along with a bell-sleeved tunic. Then I grab my purse and head out to the middle school to watch Kiara play.

It's another beautiful day, the fourth we've had thanks to the most recent warm front, so I take my time walking toward school, enjoying the downhill stroll past two neat rows of small, well-kept houses. I laugh as I stare at their lawns, a mix of Christmas lights and Thanksgiving corn stalks, left over from the week before. Just ahead I see a family outside dragging their pumpkins to the curb, the back of the SUV loaded with pine. It's a reminder of the cold to come. I've always dreaded that first day I need to wear my puffy coat for the walk to school, because once it goes on, I know I won't be warm again until spring.

But this year, with the launch of JKDesigns, winter doesn't seem as daunting. For the next few months, it'll just be me and the sewing machine—and hopefully a bundle of sales as well. My stomach flip-flops as I consider the possibilities. Maybe I'll sell tons of bags right away, maybe it'll take longer to get going. I tell myself that either way it doesn't matter, even if Kiara has already sold three headbands.

As I near the school, I spot Cameron and Lori ahead and run over to them, eager to say hello and fold into the group. I've been friends with Cam and Lori since fifth grade, when we took tennis lessons together and realized none of us was cut out for the sport. Since then, they've gotten to know Kiara, and we all eat lunch together and talk a lot during our shared classes. Yet despite this, neither Kiara nor I have hung out with them outside school in ages— they're super into music and are usually tied up with lessons. But today they're both free. Talk about lucky! I was going to come to the game no matter what, but it's much nicer to hang out with friends at the same time.

They're chatting about the boys' game when I reach them, which is happening right after the girls'. Apparently the bus holding the boys' away team just passed them, and even through the bus windows, Lori and Cam could tell that more than one of them was cute. I try to laugh along as Lori fills me in on the brief encounter, then starts evaluating the cuteness of our own players. Within seconds, this turns into a rundown of who has a crush on who.

I laugh as she continues. The one thing Lori likes more than music is gossip. Not creating it, but talking about it. Especially crushes. She even started a spreadsheet to keep track of them all! Sometimes at school it can get a little old—I'd much rather be discussing my latest sewing projects. But today I don't mind—I'm thankful for the distraction.

We reach the bleachers and I sit down between them, excited to have an afternoon out with friends. Who knows, maybe they'll even want to go to Dolce later! Before I can even ask, though, Lori kills my plans. Turns out her clarinet lesson starts right after the game.

"I'm not sure I can even stay 'til the end," she says. "Such a bummer."

Cameron nods, then starts complaining about her trumpet lesson that afternoon. *Oh well*, I think, still smiling. *At least we can have fun now*. Which is easy to do because as soon as the game starts, our team dominates. Again and again the ball bounces between girls, first to Aliyah, then Mary Beth, and then Kiara. I hold my breath as Kiara dashes down the court and scores. We all erupt into cheers. She repeats this three more times throughout the game, and each time I'm so proud that I find it hard not to stand up and scream. So instead I whoop with the crowd and clap my hands to the beat of the band as the Southfield Sharks cruise to victory against the Greenwich Tigers with a score of 63 to 52.

"That was amazing!" I say after the final buzzer. "I can't believe we're so good!"

Cameron and Lori nod and wave goodbye, then head off to their music lessons. I decide to swing by the locker room, eager to congratulate Kiara. After fighting through the crowd, I find her by the door with Aliyah and Beatrice. She runs over to me as soon as our eyes meet.

"Hey, amazing job today," I say. "You were on fire!"

"Really? You think? I feel like I missed a lot of shots."

"But you made a lot too! I'm so impressed."

"Thanks," she says, smiling. "But still, it's hard not to want to do better . . ."

"Ha, I know the feeling," I say, thinking of my failed dresses. "But really. You should be thrilled. You did great."

"Aw, well thanks so much for coming, Jas. You have no idea how nice it was to see a friendly face in the stands."

"I wasn't the only one, given how you played!"

Kiara beams, unable to hide her happiness. "Well, I hate to do this, but I gotta run. Need to shower then get into the bleachers before the boys' game. We're required to watch," she says, rolling her eyes. Though even as she does it, I can tell that she really doesn't mind.

For a moment I pause, wondering if she'll ask me to stay and watch the boys too. Not that I'm dying to watch, especially with my sketchbook and sewing projects awaiting me at home. Though if it meant I could spend more time with Kiara, I'd probably stay. But after a moment of silence, I decide the invitation isn't coming.

"I guess I'll see you later then. Monday morning?" I say.

Kiara nods. "Sorry, I'd ask you to stay and watch with us, but it's kinda a team thing. I'm really happy you came though."

"Of course. Any time."

Kiara starts to wave goodbye before stopping

mid-wave and reaching for my arm. "Hey! That reminds me. One more thing before you go."

She twirls me around until I'm facing Aliyah and Beatrice, both of whom are now talking to their parents.

"So? What do you think?"

"Think? Of what?"

"The headbands, silly!"

Biting my lip, I look at the girls again. And there I see the thin stripes of navy blue fabric poking through their hair, a small pink KM monogram a centimeter from their ears.

"Oh wow," I say, surprised at how different the headbands look from her earlier prototypes. "They look great!"

"I know, don't they? I'm making them now for the whole team. Thought maybe we could get other sports teams into it too, and maybe you could even design some bags to match . . ." Kiara's eyes dance with possibility.

"Yeah, maybe. That could work," I say. And even though I've never designed a sports bag before, right away I can see that it's a good idea. Kiara's energy spreads through me as she goes on about duffle bags and water bottle holders and matching ribbons.

"It'd be a great way to combine interests, don't you think?"

"Definitely," I say. "Wanna come over tomorrow? Maybe we can work on some of the plans. I can't believe break's only two weeks away. In two weeks, JKDesigns will be a reality!"

"Yeah, I know! Though I'm busy tomorrow. But I'll see you Monday. On the way to school?"

"Yeah, sure," I say.

"Sounds fabulous. And I'd say we could talk in science, but after what happened this morning, I don't think there'll be time for much girl talk."

I raise my brow. "Why?"

"He asked to join our group."

"Carter?"

"Yup. Before warm-ups. He found me and asked if he could partner with us. Since Teddy switched classes last week."

"And then there were three," I say.

Kiara shrugs. "Guess so! All right then. Tick tock, girl," she says.

But instead of extending her hand for a shake, she slips away toward Aliyah and Beatrice, who are already yelling for her to join them.

Chapter Four
Fashion Disaster

The next day, Sunday, I spend most of the day in my room, draping fabric and trying to get this custom pattern thing right. I turn up the music and belt out my favorite playlist as I pin the fabric I'm using to make my dress pattern onto my dress form. It's a bright yellow polka-dot cotton—the cheapest fabric I could find. When my playlist begins its second loop, I'm finally ready to slip the pinned-together dress off the form and try it on. I cross my fingers and breathe in as I slip it over my head.

And then I sigh. Once again, it's too small.

"Of course," I say, taking it off. I place it back on the form, then let out the pins by an inch all around.

This time my practice dress hangs off me—way too big. I frown, once again wishing I had enough money to buy myself one of those fancy dress forms where you can adjust the size.

And that's when the idea strikes. Excited, I take my measurements again. Then I look around my room, finally eyeing an old pillow. Biting down on my lip, I grab it and rip it open, gathering up the stuffing buried inside. With a roll of duct tape in one hand, I use the other to spread the stuffing across the dress form's hips until they are two inches wider, and actually my size.

"There, that should work," I say aloud.

I re-pin my fabric to the dress form in my original design and try it on. This time it fits!

"Yes!" I say, dancing around the room. "Maybe this one will work!"

I take my pinned dress and draw on all the pencil lines—where to place zippers and seams and darts—then unpin the fabric until I have a pile of pieces making up the top, the skirt, and the sleeves. I pin these to the actual fabric for my final dress (a pretty pink-and-white-stripe pattern), then cut it.

Finally, I start to sew, using the hand-me-down

machine Mom gave me last Christmas. I stop once I've put together the top part. Too excited to wait for the whole dress, I tear it off the machine and throw it over my head.

And it's too small. Still. Too. Small. Even though the pinned pattern pieces fit.

I fight the urge to scream as I ball up yet another wad of pink for the trash.

"That's it! I'm never gonna get this," I say.

"Sounds like someone needs a break," I hear Abuela say.

I turn around to see her standing by the door, an apron tied around her waist.

"Abuela!" I say, glad for the distraction. "I didn't know you were cooking today."

She shrugs. "It's Sunday. A good day for chicken stew. Hungry?"

My stomach growls. "Definitely."

I throw down my scissors and hop up, ready to join her at the door. But before I can, I see her walking around my dress form.

"In my day we didn't use patterns. Did everything up here," she says, pointing to her head. "I used to be able to make a shirt in thirty minutes. Would just take the old one, trace it onto the fabric and cut. Then a few minutes with the needle and that was that. One, two, three."

I sigh, having heard the story before. Abuela was never much of a fashion designer, but before her eyesight got bad she was an expert seamstress, making much of her family's clothes.

"Yeah. I don't know what I'm doing wrong," I say.

She pulls my pink top out of the trash and looks it over. "This for you?"

I nod.

"Too small."

"I know. I think I messed up the cutting."

"You have to allow for that," she says. "Don't just add for seams. Add for cutting too. You can always adjust fit later."

"Isn't that more work?" I ask.

She shrugs. "Maybe, but you can always make smaller. But making it bigger . . ." She shakes her head.

I mentally file away the tip as she stands up. "Now let's go. Stew's ready and no one else is home. Only thing I hate more than cold stew is eating alone."

I laugh. "They'll be back later tonight," I say,

reminding Abuela of the twins' indoor baseball tournament. She just rolls her eyes—if there is one thing Abuela doesn't get, it's sports—and guides me to the kitchen.

An hour later I'm back in my room with my fabric, stomach full. But my mind keeps drifting—winter break, and the launch of JKDesigns, is only two weeks away. As much as I'd like to work on getting my dress right, I need to finish up my bags. Reaching for my basket of prototypes, I wonder if I should turn one of my totes into more of a sports bag, like Kiara mentioned yesterday. But having never played sports myself, I have no idea what features the bags need. And would they vary for different sports? Perplexed, I run a few searches on Etsy but am overwhelmed with results. *Maybe I should ask the twins*, I think, as I hear them pounding around again downstairs. But if I go downstairs, I'll be stuck there for hours, listening to every detail of the day's events. So instead I decide to call it an early night. Kiara and I can talk about it tomorrow on the walk to school.

I wake the next morning with renewed energy, a list of questions about sports bags queued up in my head. As I reach for my backpack, my new messenger bag catches my eye. And even though the beading's still not perfect, I decide I'm in too good a mood to leave it behind. Within minutes, I have my books transferred and I'm ready to show off my sparkling new messenger bag to Kiara, along with my ideas on sports bags.

But when I reach our meeting spot, Kiara isn't alone.

"Hey girl, you know Mary Beth," she says, waving me over.

"Uh, yeah, of course," I say, trying to hide my disappointment. "Um, how are you guys?"

"Did you know she lives just off Ridgeway?" Kiara says, pointing to the road intersecting ours. "She's only two blocks up."

"Oh cool," I say, readjusting my messenger bag as we start walking. Has Kiara even noticed it? Her eyes are focused on Mary Beth.

"I usually cut the back way through the woods," says Mary Beth, "but when Kiara told me she was gonna rehash her convo with Carter, I figured I couldn't miss it." She giggles as she rubs her hands together for warmth. The weather has turned cold overnight, and my dreaded puffy coat is now zipped up to my chin.

"Oh yeah, I can't wait to hear either. This was Saturday, right? When he asked to join our lab group?" I say, remembering what Kiara said after the basketball game.

"No, not *that*," Mary Beth says. "Right Ki, I mean, I was there for *that*. I thought you were gonna tell us about *last night*?"

"What was last night?" I ask.

"Carter asked her to call him. After the team lunch. He gave her his number!"

Team lunch? With Carter? And Mary Beth? A pit forms in my stomach.

"Really? Uh, wow," I say.

"I know, right? I couldn't believe it," says Kiara. "I meant to text you about it, but then it got late and I figured I'd just tell you today on the walk. But God, I feel like I've been shaking ever since. The whole thing is just so *rich*!" Kiara's voice rises and falls like a hummingbird as she dances across the asphalt.

"OhmiGod it's so *rich*! She wouldn't even fill me in first!" says Mary Beth.

I nod and smile as Mary Beth waves her hands in unison with Kiara's and I try to ignore the gurgling in my stomach. Even though I know Sunday's event was a team lunch, I can't help but feel left out of something fun. Or *rich*, as Kiara and Mary Beth would say. I sigh under my breath as I stare up at the few remaining leaves still clinging to the maples. Even the words they use are different. How am I supposed to fit in?

Yet I force myself to smile as Kiara starts dissecting her phone call, and I wonder the whole time if Kiara really is sharing her new life with me after all. Some days she tells me everything, other days nothing. She's always enthusiastic when I text her with updates on my bags or ask homework questions, but lately her responses have been short. More emojis, less conversation. And now she hasn't even noticed my new messenger bag. I breathe in deep. *Calm down, Jas*, I tell myself. *She just has a lot going on*. But watching her dance down the street, I can't help but wish I had as much going on too.

"So then, get this, Jas." Kiara grabs my hand, snapping me back to the conversation. "Carter actually asked if I could make him one too!"

"Wait. Make him what? A headband?" I say.

"Yes! Isn't that hilarious?"

"OhmiGod that's crazy!" says Mary Beth.

"Yeah," I say. "What would he do with it? Wear it?"

"Well, he does have all those curls," says Mary Beth. "Maybe they've been getting in the way. Don't want him having to squint to see you." She gives Kiara a nudge.

Kiara's face reddens. "Hey, cut it out! I think he was just trying to be supportive."

"And tell you he likes you," Mary Beth says.

"You think?"

"You think!" Mary Beth says.

I laugh and nod along. The conversation is moving too fast for me to jump in.

But then Kiara turns to me. "What do you think, Jas?"

I bite down on my lip. Knowing Carter only from afar, it doesn't seem fair to answer. But with Mary Beth so sure and Kiara so excited, I decide it's safest to agree.

"Seems like he definitely likes you," I say. "A lot."

Kiara giggles just as the red brick exterior of Southfield Middle comes into focus. "Well, thank God, because all I keep thinking about are those curls!"

I laugh along with Kiara and Mary Beth as the first bell chimes overhead.

"See you at lunch?" Mary Beth calls to Kiara.

"Of course—see you both then," she says.

We both nod. Lately Kiara's been sitting with me and Cam and Lori just long enough to devour her sandwich. Then she spends the rest of lunch "visiting" with the basketball table. Cam and Lori don't really seem to care—Lori has started using lunch to update her crush sheet. But it's left me really missing my best friend.

Before we part ways, Kiara turns to me and I wonder if she's going to say something about my bag. But it turns out her mind is still on Carter. "Now if only we could fast forward to science," she says.

"I know," I say, then pause, wanting her to smile and laugh with me like she used to, like she's been doing with Mary Beth. So, mustering up some enthusiasm, I reach for Kiara's arm. "That'd be *rich*," I say.

Kiara's eyes light up and relief courses through my veins. "I know. I bet he'll even sit at our science table now. You know, since we're all partners."

She shoots me a wink and I keep laughing, even though the thought of Carter at our table makes me nervous—because right now Kiara and Mary Beth and I are all laughing together. *Maybe I can fit in with these basketball girls yet,* I think, envisioning a future where we're all friends. I smile as I walk away, the remnants of saying my first *rich* still caught in my teeth. I swirl it around a little, trying to get used to it, this new word in this new world of Kiara. By the time I reach social studies class, I decide I like it. Today will be rich. Today will be grand.

Yet I struggle to focus as Mr. Worthington instructs us to open our books to the chapter on China. Usually I love this class, but today Mr. Worthington's energy just distracts me, like a fly buzzing around my food. My mind jumps from China to my new sports bag idea and then to Kiara and back again. And as the day goes on, the closer we get to science, the antsier I get. By the end of English, I'm counting down the minutes.

And then it's time. As I walk toward science, I wonder how nervous Kiara is, knowing she's about to sit next to her crush. I brush away the thought as I swing my new messenger bag into my arms and start digging for my Chap Stick. I run it against my lips, then throw it back into my bag, taking a moment to inspect my beadwork. It looks good! So far, the bag seems to be working well. It fits all my books, but isn't too bulky when I'm walking down the halls. Plus, the bright colors and sparkling beads really make it pop.

Weaving through the congested hallway, I scan the crowd for any familiar faces.

And that's when I see him. Someone new. Walking to my right. Strolling, really. Head back, dark tan skin, and piercing blue eyes shining through the shadows cast by his chewed-up baseball cap. He's wearing a faded Bruce Springsteen concert T-shirt. *Old school*, I think, eyeing the shirt's frayed hems, the gray threads hanging from them almost a perfect match to the ones on his hat. He's staring out straight ahead smiling, and for a second our eyes meet. My heart races as he tips his head.

"Hey," he says, moving his hand off his backpack strap just long enough to give a little wave.

My cheeks burning, I eke out a "Hi" just before he ambles by.

Who was that? I wonder, my palms sweaty. *And why have I never seen him before?* My heart is thudding heavily. Is this how Kiara feels about Carter? Because, wow—now I get it.

I move to the side of the hall, then turn and try to spot him again, but he's been swallowed up in the crowd. My mind races as I consider the possibilities. Is he a seventh grader? I need to ask Kiara. Or sign on to FriendChat. See if I can recognize his profile picture in any of my friends' feeds. But of course I can't do any of that now—science awaits. With Kiara and Carter. So, no girl talk allowed.

I sigh, then readjust my messenger bag, ready to brave class. Then I hear a familiar voice behind me.

"Did you see her bag today? I mean, I know she's your friend and everything, but it was kinda ridiculous," it says.

I freeze as kids brush past me.

That voice. Those words.

It's Mary Beth. Talking about a bag. Which sounds a lot like mine.

Chapter Five

ALL ALONE

My stomach flips as I look for a place to hide, my mind already replaying the conversation I had with her and Kiara earlier, the one where I thought we'd gotten along as friends. Was she just pretending the whole time?

I'm right by a dark, empty classroom, so I bolt inside and crouch there in the dark. The door isn't all the way closed, and through the crack I can see Mary Beth standing and laughing outside the science room with Kiara and Aliyah. I wait and listen for Kiara's response. Kiara loves my bags. She'll come to my defense, right?

But then, she doesn't.

"Yeah, I know," I hear her say. "She's really into this whole fashion design thing, but her bags are just so *juvenile*. I've tried to push her to make other things, but what can I say? In her mind, sparkles and neon are cool."

What?

Shaking, I collapse onto the ground and will myself not to cry. How can she say that? How can she think that? Kiara! My very best friend! Talking behind my back! Does she really think my bags are so awful? Why has she never said anything to me before? And since when is Kiara the type of girl to talk about anybody, let alone her best friend?

I watch Kiara and her basketball friends giggling. Their conversation has moved on, to science class and sitting next to Carter.

I wipe the sweat off my forehead and force myself to stand back up. I tell myself I must've heard wrong. That I must've missed something vital said earlier in the conversation. That there's no way they're really talking about me.

But a moment later, I hear Aliyah. "I'm sorry, but she really is an odd duck," she says. "Does she even play a sport? What do you guys do together, anyway?"

Kiara sighs. "Oh who knows? We're friends because our moms are friends. She's just someone I have to be nice to."

"Ah, gotcha. I've got one of those too," says Mary Beth. "I call her my face friend, because I have to be nice to her face."

There's no doubt who they are talking about now. I think of our last sleepover, of JKDesigns, and all Kiara's promises that even with basketball, we'd still have time together. Of our secret handshake. The unspoken promise that we'd always be friends.

Tick tock. Tick tock.

I think I'm gonna be sick.

I dash out of the empty classroom and head toward the nurse's station just as the bell rings. A few steps in, I hear Kiara.

"Oh shoot," she says. "Jasmine? Hey Jas, wait up—I can explain . . ."

But I don't stop. I've done enough waiting.

And besides, there's nothing she can say that can repair the hole she's just blown in our friendship. Nothing that will convince me she's not lying to my face. So instead I keep running. Down the science wing. Past the English rooms. All the way to the main hall.

Focus. Breathe. Don't cry. I repeat this over and over as the nurse's office comes into view. I'll say I'm sick. Call Mom. Go home. But when I turn the corner, I see there's a line outside the office and some eighth graders snickering about a bad batch of chili at lunch.

Just my luck, I think. I still need to escape, so I slip out the back exit, find a bench, and sit. When I'm sure I'm alone, I let myself cry. Big, salty, heaving tears. They hit me in waves, coming and going as my mind swirls. I still can't believe Kiara could say that about me.

Only she did. And she knew I heard her. She yelled after me in the hall.

And then she didn't follow me.

She went to class. Carter is probably with her now, sitting in my seat.

Head spinning, I reach for my phone. I need to talk to someone. But who? What if Lori and Cameron feel the same way about my bags as Kiara? What if Mom gets angry at Kiara and says something to Mrs. Murphy? That could shut down JKDesigns for good. But then, is there even a shop to shut down? How can I ever face Kiara again?

Another wave of nausea overtakes me as I stand up and glance toward the street. School's in session for another thirty minutes, and there's a crossing guard checking dismissal passes at the main exit. But there's a path behind the school that leads to my neighborhood. I get low and walk toward it, breaking into a run when I'm close. When I feel the dirt beneath my feet, I relax, walking the rest of the way in silence. My eyes are dry and itchy now, empty of tears. I focus on my footsteps instead of thinking.

At home, I run up to my room, only retreating downstairs for dinner. With winter break so close, school is busy with tests and projects and last-minute assignments, so I just tell my parents I'm overwhelmed with homework when they ask what's wrong. And then I spend the rest of the night worrying about what to say to Kiara when I see her tomorrow morning on the corner.

Only the next morning, she's not there. Nor the one after that. And at lunch, I find she's moved to the girls' basketball table full time, leaving me to mumble something about the basketball coach wanting the team to spend more time together when Lori and Cameron ask about it. I don't even see her much in science class, because now she's always the last into class and the first to leave, usually with Carter. And we don't sit together anymore—Carter's request to join our group was apparently denied on account of me and him both having the best grades in the class. So now, instead, our lab partners got switched completely. Kiara sits with Carter and I sit in the back with Noah, who'd rather be making paper footballs than paying attention to anything going on in class. Whenever I look Kiara's way, she stares at the ground or pretends to be deep in concentration, acting like I'm not there at all.

A whole week passes without a word from Kiara. At first, I keep waiting for her to reappear, at my locker, or on the street corner, or even at Dolce. But every time I turn, expecting to hear her throaty "Hey girl," she's never there. I guess our friendship is really over.

Turns out, losing your best friend right before the holidays is pretty awful—every special event is a reminder of what's happened. Like on Friday, when the student council delivered the peppermint grams in seventh period, and for the first time there wasn't one with my name on it. And then on Sunday when I signed on to FriendChat and saw tons of pictures from this big party at Aliyah's house. Kiara was in a bunch of them with Carter. I wonder if they're going out now.

Brushing the thought aside, I head for science. It's finally the last day of school before break, and science is my last class of the last day. In forty-five minutes, I'll be free for ten whole days. Normally, I'd be ecstatic at so much free time—but now, those long empty days do not sound appealing. Because there's no JKDesigns to launch. And we're not going on any big ski vacation or trip to some tropical island. My break is going to be just a lot of babysitting the twins and helping Abuela with her holiday baking and wondering what went wrong with Kiara. I guess I could work on my patterns, too, but just the thought of designing anything makes my head hurt.

When the classroom door comes into view, I take a deep breath, trying to prepare myself for Noah's onslaught of sports trivia. Then I feel a tap from behind. It's Lori, sucking away on a peppermint stick.

"Hey Jas, we've missed you at lunch this week," she says.

I force a smile and try to laugh. "Oh yeah, sorry about that. I've been finishing up some social studies extra credit," I say. After the first day Kiara abandoned our lunch table, I've been skipping the cafeteria for any excuse I can think of. Not that I don't like Lori and Cameron, but seeing Kiara smiling a few tables down can be a lot to take.

"Cam mentioned something about that. But still we missed you. After the peppermint grams, we've had a lot of crushes to update. I need to fill you in!"

"Yeah, I heard," I say. "Maybe we can get together over break."

"Maybe," she says. "Though next week I've got this piano camp every day. And then we're going to visit family in Ohio . . . but after break maybe. Or maybe after winter concert, when rehearsals calm down."

"Yeah sure," I say, knowing the odds of us hanging out are small.

"But anyway, I know we don't have much time, but I heard this thing last weekend and it's been bothering me."

"Okay."

"It's just, I know that you and Kiara have been close forever. And I know she stopped sitting with us at lunch, but you said that was because of basketball."

"Right. That's what she told me, anyway," I say.

"Yeah, same. I texted her about peppermint grams—I just had to get the details about her and Carter!" she says.

"Oh yeah, definitely," I say, relieved to hear Kiara went along with my story, yet sad to know Lori's still talking to my old best friend.

"But anyway, when we texted the other night, everything seemed totally normal. I told her I was bummed she had to sit with the basketball girls at lunch and she said she was sad too. So then when I heard this thing the other day, well it was all kinda shocking. But is it true? That you and Kiara aren't friends anymore?"

Her words hit me like a punch to the stomach.

"Wait. What?" I say. It stings to hear her say the truth out loud. And if Kiara didn't say anything, then who did? My knees begin to shake as Lori reaches for my hand.

"You and Kiara. That's why she's not sitting with us, isn't it? And why you've had all those extra credit projects during lunch?"

My cheeks burn as my head starts to spin. "I . . . I . . . who said that?"

Lori frowns. "Aliyah. She said you got into a big fight about Kiara playing basketball. That you were, uh, jealous? And made a big scene about it?"

"She said that? To you?" My heart pounds as I try to control my breathing.

"No, not to me. Cameron overheard it. At Aliyah's party on Saturday."

"Cameron was there?"

Lori frowns. "Oh, we only got invited because we all share homeroom. I'm sure you would've been asked too, if not because of—well, you know."

So Lori was there too. My voice creeps higher as I try to stay calm.

"Okay, well that's not what happened! I don't know. I never said anything to Kiara. Nothing at all! And I certainly never made a scene! I can't believe they're saying this," I say in a rush. "Kiara was the one who was saying mean stuff about *me*! I overheard her in the hall, and she saw. And then—then she just started ignoring me, and never apologized or explained or anything. And now she's spreading rumors? About me being jealous? It's not fair!" The tears spill over onto my blue plaid shirt.

Lori's arms wrap around me. "I'm sorry," she says.

"I had a feeling it wasn't true. I couldn't imagine you ever making a scene. But I thought you'd wanna know what people were saying. And if you ever want to talk, just text me. I'm not home most nights until after eight, and then I'm usually doing homework, but after that I'm all yours . . ."

"Thanks," I say, wiping my eyes on my arm. Even though we both know I'll never text her that late, it feels good to hear her offer.

"Well, I'm sorry to dump all this and run, but I gotta go. And seriously, don't worry about Kiara. It's probably just a misunderstanding or something. I'm sure it'll all blow over soon."

I shake my head. "Maybe," I say.

She smiles. "Don't worry. It will. And we'll hang out. After the concert. Okay?"

"Yeah, sounds great," I say, even though I feel anything but great.

The bell rings and the last thing I want to do is enter that classroom, but I do, surprised to see Kiara already there. For a moment I debate stopping at her desk and telling her exactly what I think of her and her new friends, but at the last second I chicken out. Instead I stare right at her as I pass by, letting the anger bounce from my eyes to hers. She brings her hand to her face and shuffles the papers on her desk before turning back to Carter, a wide grin hiding any sign that she even noticed me.

Without a word, I walk straight ahead and sit down. I feel naked sitting there at my table, as if everyone can see right through my skin to my thoughts. Does everybody think I'm jealous of Kiara? Who did she tell that to? And why? Maybe she could tell I was sad about being left out, but why act like this? Was I not a good enough friend?

I try to shake the thoughts away, but the pain of Kiara's betrayal stings like a burn. I can feel the heat radiating from my cheeks as I scan the classroom, trying to spot anyone looking at me. But of course there's nothing I can do about it if they are, and nowhere I can go. So, breathing in deep, I take a cue from Kiara and pretend that nothing's wrong until the bell finally rings and class is over. Then I disappear out into the street and the empty days of winter break, wrapped up tight in my puffy coat.

Chapter Six
The Flyer

"Come on, honey, are you sure you don't want to go with me? I'm headed to the fabric store after I drop the boys," Mom says, lingering in the doorway of my room. I'm in the home stretch of winter break now—just two more long, boring days to go—and since Christmas last weekend, I have barely left the house. Lucky for me, Santa thought to fill my stocking with books. As much as I've missed my sewing, every time I've pulled out my dress patterns or tried to work on my bags, I have felt a little sick.

"I told you, I'm done with all that. No more fashion design."

Mom sighs. "And let me guess. You still don't want

to talk about it. Well, you know you can't hide from me forever."

I frown. Ever since I stopped hanging out with Kiara, Mom's been on my case. How she noticed, I'm not even sure, given that Kiara wasn't around much lately because of basketball anyway. But then, she does talk a lot to Kiara's mom, so maybe she mentioned something—not that I can imagine Kiara telling her mom about what's really going on, either. But somehow, Mom figured out I was upset and has been hounding me ever since. I start to resist her pleas again, but I can tell from her pursed lips that my week of moping has started to really worry her. Maybe it's time to give in.

"Fine. If you really want to know," I say.

"I do, honey. I really do. Tell me about it."

I nod. "Well then, I guess it all happened a couple weeks before break . . . I heard Kiara and her basketball friends talking in the hall. They were . . . they were ripping apart the new bag I made and saying I've got awful taste. And then Kiara was saying she was just nice to me because she had to be. And then some other girls at school overheard rumors that Kiara was telling everyone *I* was the one talking about *her* because I was jealous of basketball, only I never said anything!"

The words I've locked away for weeks spill out faster than the tears as I bury my head into Mom's lap.

"All this time I thought we were friends! We were never really friends at all," I say between heaves.

Mom rubs my back, and lets the tears fall. I stare down at my purple comforter and try to focus on its geometric pattern, hoping it will help me calm down. But I still feel sick, even as the tears slow.

For a moment, neither of us speaks.

Then Mom shifts her weight and breathes in.

"You know, honey, growing up is tough," she says. "Everyone's jostling around, trying on new identities, seeing what fits and throwing out what doesn't. Right now, Kiara seems determined to get these basketball girls to like her. Though let me tell you, if these girls are so quick to make fun of you, they'll never be her real friends. People who put down others are too insecure to have real friends. And as soon as they feel threatened by Kiara, they'll be talking about her. Just you wait."

"But Kiara . . . I just never thought she would be that way. I mean, how could she say that about me? And then twist it around to her friends?"

Mom shakes her head. "I don't know. I really don't. But the important thing is you don't take it to heart. You are still the same incredibly talented and hard-working girl today as you were before she said those nasty things. And your bags are gorgeous! So many beautiful details and intricate stitching. They're works of art! And it's not just me who sees it. Every time I see Ms. Chloe, she goes on and on about how talented you are."

"But what am I supposed to do? Kiara's mom's the one with the fancy camera! She was gonna help us start the shop!"

"Well, why don't I run down the street and borrow it from her? I don't even have to tell her what we're doing. Or, we can go down to Ms. Chloe's and use hers. She's always uploading things to Etsy. I'm sure she can teach us."

My eyes widen at the thought, but then I shake it away. "No. No more bags. No more Ms. Chloe. I need a break."

Mom nods. "Fair enough. But I'm not gonna let you wither away in here all winter like some dried-out prune. If you don't want to sew, that's fine, but then you need to choose another activity."

"Another activity? No! Please, can't I just take a break?"

"From your bags, yes. But not from life. Now throw on some clothes. I have to drop the boys at practice, but when I get back here, you and I are going to the movies. No complaining."

"Fine," I say.

"Great!"

I gather a towel and head to the shower as the front door slams, amazed at how Mom can so quickly move from outraged at Kiara to invigorated by her new plan. But then, I guess that's Mom. She's always more of a doer than a thinker. Me, I'd rather live with my thoughts for a while before deciding what to do about them. But Mom never even takes time to pause. Part of me hopes her busy schedule will keep her from worrying too much about mine. But that's the other thing about Mom—once she's put her mind to something, she rarely changes course.

So I'm not surprised the next afternoon when she barges into my room, interrupting my hundredth futile mystery boy FriendChat search, with the town Parks and Rec flyer in hand.

"I've got it! The perfect activity for you! In fact, it's

so perfect I can't believe I didn't think of it before!" Mom says, as I minimize my laptop screen.

"So I guess you haven't forgotten," I say.

Mom laughs. "Of course not! And look here! Salsa dancing!"

"Salsa dancing?"

"Yes!" Mom is bubbling over with excitement now, dancing around my room, busting out moves I've never seen. "You can be just like me. Come to think of it, I started dancing right around the time I was your age. Back in Texas, salsa was huge . . ."

I roll my eyes as Mom's eyes glaze over, her mind clearly back in Houston, years before she met my Yankee dad and moved up north. Even though I've seen her old pictures and videos, her long hair and slender legs shaking and shimmying up on the stage, it seems weird to imagine her as any younger than she is now.

But even harder to imagine is me doing any of that shaking business.

I look Mom in the eyes and shake my head. "No. Not a chance. Dancing is *so* not my thing."

"Come on, it's perfect!" Mom looks down at the flyer. "See here? They meet every Friday night for an hour . . . Oh, wait. Uh-oh. It says it's for ages thirteen and up."

Whew. "Well that's that then," I say. "I'm too young! I can't do it."

"Shoot," Mom says, deflated. "I really think you would've liked it."

"Yeah, well, I guess I'll just have to do something else."

Mom nods, her eyes already back to the flyer. "Let's see. There's karate, and gymnastics, but I don't think they have any classes for your age group. And then there are swimming lessons at the beach . . . but that's not 'til summer. Oh—wait! This looks interesting."

Uh-oh. I cringe as the twinkle returns to Mom's eyes.

"What is it?" I ask, unsure I'm ready for the answer.

"Drama club!"

"Drama club?"

"Yes!" says Mom, clapping her hands. "Oh this is perfect! It says right here it's just for middle schoolers. Starts in January and runs through March. And it all culminates with a production of their very own version of *Cinderella*, on stage at the high school!"

"Drama club?" I say again. "But I can't act."

"That's only because you've never tried."

"But I hate crowds. And talking to groups. I can't get up there on stage!"

"Well, that's what the class is for, honey. To teach you all that! But this will be great. Remember back in elementary school, how much you enjoyed choir? You always had the sweetest singing voice . . ."

I get up from my desk and snatch the flyer from Mom's hands. "Isn't there something else I can try? *Anything* else?"

Mom shrugs. "Would you rather try a sport? Maybe softball. Or lacrosse . . ."

I shake my head. Sports have never been my thing.

"Then drama club."

"Mom, I really don't know . . ."

"Okay. How about this? Just give it a try. Three classes. You go to three classes and hate it, then we'll go back to the flyer and find something else that starts in the spring. But no quitting until you've given it a fair shot, all right?"

"Fine," I say.

"Great!" Mom says. "I can see it now . . . 'Introducing Jasmine Wilson in the part of Cinderella!'"

I roll my eyes. "You know I'm not gonna get the lead," I say.

"I know nothing of the sort. In fact, all I know is you need to get dressed. The first class starts in an hour."

"What? But it's vacation! And a Saturday!"

"Well, it says here they usually meet Wednesdays after school. But the first one is today. An introductory meeting."

"But I'm not ready!" I say.

Mom smiles. "You won't be any more prepared on Wednesday."

"At least I'd have time to figure out what to wear."

Mom throws me a towel and turns to my closet.

"Better get cracking," she says.

Shaking, I bolt to the bathroom. I turn the water up as hot as it goes and let it scald my skin as I think of what's just happened. In ten minutes I've gone from sitting on my bed obsessing over FriendChat to being forced into drama club. Part of me wants to cry, the other part is sick with nerves. Though there's also a part that's excited to have a reason to get dressed. I cling to that as I throw on my favorite jeans and sweater combo before running downstairs.

"Oh look at you. Just beautiful," Mom says.

"Right," I say, lips trembling.

"Don't worry, it'll be fine," she says.

"And if it's not?"

"Then we'll find something else. Remember, just give it a few classes."

I nod as Mom leaves me at the door. There I zip on my boots and grab the house key from its hook. Then I hesitate. Dangling there next to my shabby brown purse is my new messenger bag. The same one that got me into this mess in the first place. Breathing in, I snatch it. *Maybe this time it'll bring good luck*, I think. Then I give Mom a kiss, yell goodbye to Abuela—like always she's on the computer, chatting with her sister—and start trekking to the high school, a block up the road from Southfield Middle.

As the cold soaks through my coat, I wonder whether I should've just taken up Mom on her offer to start my Etsy shop. I could be back at Ms. Chloe's place right now, cloves and cinnamon calming my electric nerves. But it's too late for any of that now. Mom's already emailed to register me for the class. Miss Tabitha has already written back, saying she's excited to have me. And I've already run three blocks in boots. I've gone from zero to sixty in an hour. And as scared as I am, I'm surprised to find that buried beneath my apprehension is a little excitement too. For the first time since I can remember, I'll be doing something new. I laugh as the first smile in weeks takes over my face. Ready or not, it's time for me to start my own adventure.

Chapter Seven
BREAK A LEG

I enter the auditorium in a daze, my eyes blinking as they adjust to the bright lights shining over the stage. The chairs beside me are empty and it takes a moment before I notice the crowd gathered down below, filling the first three rows of seats. In front and above, moving under the bright lights on stage, is a woman I assume is Miss Tabitha. She's swaying back and forth to some show tune playing in the background as kids file into their seats.

For a moment, I freeze, remembering the lies Kiara told about me at Aliyah's party. What if some theater kids were there too? What if everyone here has heard the gossip? Will they hear my name and think I'm some crazy jealous crybaby? I bite down on my lip as I shuffle down the aisle. *Kiara and Aliyah would never hang out with theater kids*, I tell myself as I grab a seat in the still-empty fourth row. They only hang out with kids who do sports. *And those they share homeroom with*, I think, with a shudder. My cheeks on fire, I slump down low and scan the room as Miss Tabitha tells us we'll be starting in just a few more minutes. There are more kids than I expected, easily thirty or forty, yet not a single face looks familiar. I decide this is a good thing. They probably have enough gossip of their own to keep them busy.

As the lights flash—a sign that we'll be starting soon—a group of girls sits down next to me. Before they've taken off their jackets they're whispering among themselves, giggling about scenery and costumes and auditions. *Geez, what have I agreed to?* I wonder, trying to imagine myself up on stage. I thought this was a club, not a competition. I sink even lower as I try to avoid my new seatmates. Deep in conversation, they don't seem to notice me.

About a minute later, Miss Tabitha claps out a beat and asks the audience to follow her lead. Together we clap back her pattern, pounding out the rhythm until there is no more chatter. Once the room is silent, Miss Tabitha begins.

"Ladies and gentlemen, good afternoon!" she begins, sounding a little like a circus announcer. "It is so great to see so many faces—both old and new. As you know, today is the first meeting of this year's Southfield Middle Drama Club. I am so excited to have you all here! Most of today will be informational, but I promise I will get you into groups toward the end so you can begin getting to know each other and preparing for auditions."

I gulp at yet another mention of auditions. *Do I really have to do this?* I think, as Miss Tabitha dives into the rehearsal schedule and performance dates.

After a minute she pauses and looks out into the crowd. "So, any questions?"

Yeah, how do I get out of here? I think.

When no hands go up, she continues. "Great, then we're going to begin by breaking into two groups. Those here for stage crew and production, please grab your things and head to Room 102 with Mr. Hart. The rest of you, hang tight."

My throat tightens as almost half the auditorium empties. For a moment I wonder if I should follow the kids leaving for stage crew—certainly anything behind the scenes sounds better than being in the spotlight—but the kids leaving seem to know each other better than the ones staying. Afraid of looking even more out of place, I decide it's safer to stay in my seat. So I dig my nails into the chair arms as I try to shed the nerves flooding my body.

As the seats around me empty, Miss Tabitha waves to those of us remaining, encouraging us to move in closer to the stage. Hands shaking, I grab my bag and move down to the first row. Once we're all seated, Miss Tabitha starts again.

"Great, thanks guys. Whew, it looks like we're going to have a great group this year. *Cinderella* is one of my favorite plays, it's always just so much fun to perform on stage. But before I get ahead of myself, I do want to go over how auditions are gonna run. There are going to be a few changes this year, so everyone pay attention . . ."

Miss Tabitha's voice rises and falls like a cresting wave as she flits around the room like an energetic fairy. She's tiny, probably shorter than some of the girls in our class, but with silver-white hair that makes it clear she's closer in age to our parents than to us. Her excitement seems genuine as she begins to delve into the audition process, yet I find it hard to focus on anything she says. Because what she's said already is terrifying. One meeting a week for the first month, followed by three rehearsals a week toward the end. And then two weekends of performances! And that's all if I survive these auditions, which were definitely left out of the two-paragraph description in the Parks and Rec flyer. Once again, I debate getting up and leaving, but now that I'm crammed into the first row, there's no way to escape without making a scene.

"So how does that sound? Easy, right?" Miss Tabitha asks. "Again, just like last year, auditions will include both singing and acting out a scene. The biggest change is that this year we're going to let you choose your own audition song. I suggest you all go home and start looking at songs tonight. The sooner you choose one, the longer you'll have to prepare. And remember, show tunes work best since you'll be auditioning a cappella, without any music. As for the scene you'll be performing, it's included in the packet you'll get before you leave. Girls will be reading the part of Cinderella, boys will be reading for Prince Charming."

The audience erupts in giggles and groans as Miss Tabitha winks to the audience. "Now, now, I promise you, it isn't the kissing scene. So don't get too excited."

Again, the kids around me laugh. Most seem as relaxed as Miss Tabitha, and I wonder if I'm the only one who hasn't done this before.

"In fact, I thought it would be helpful to have a brief scene demonstration just so you all know what we're looking for on audition day. So I've chosen two of our veteran performers here to help act out a scene—this one's different from the one you'll be doing, but it should give you an idea of what to focus on when practicing. So please, a big round of applause for Ava and Courtney. They're going to be acting out a short scene between the two stepsisters."

Two girls jump to their feet and head toward the stage to thunderous applause and whistles. On first glance, neither girl is familiar. *Probably eighth graders*, I think, as they join Miss Tabitha under the lights. But when they turn to us I realize I do know Courtney. Courtney Silver, the wide-eyed redhead who was in most of my classes last year. She was always nice but seemed quiet, so I'm shocked when she jumps into character, her demeanor loud and boisterous.

Her sharp emotion pulls me in right away, as she pretends to fumble with an invisible dress right in front of her, yelling that she has nothing to wear to the royal ball. I watch as she pretends to throw it on the ground and stomp on it, before turning to the second girl, Ava.

As soon as Ava moves into the spotlight, it seems obvious that she is the star. She's thin and tall with impeccable posture, making her look even taller and thinner. Her dark skin is flawless, not a pimple or blemish anywhere, and her long hair is braided in hundreds of tiny braids that she's woven into a bun high on the top of her head, almost like a ballerina would wear. Her voice is deep and clear, and her movements on stage just seem so natural. While Courtney's performance is captivating, Ava's is so believable that within seconds I forget that she's a student at all. In that moment, she is Anastasia, and she better look good for that ball.

"Whoa, she's amazing," I say under my breath, unaware that I've even spoken.

The girl next to me leans in. "That's Ava Cantor. She's super talented. Last summer she had a small part in a Broadway show!"

"Seriously?" I say.

"I know. Tough act to follow, right?"

"I'll say."

"Don't worry though. Miss Tabitha doesn't expect that from everyone."

I nod as the girl leans back into her seat, turning to giggle with the guy on her right. And leaving me to sweat it out alone as Courtney and Ava dazzle on stage.

At the end of the scene, after the cheering and clapping has died down, Miss Tabitha returns to the stage.

"Thank you again, Ava and Courtney! Now I hope that was as helpful as it was fun to watch. I know auditions can be scary, especially if it's your first time, but remember we're not looking for perfection. We understand that you're nervous and you might forget a line. What we're really looking for is your ability to be that character. So when practicing, put yourself in your character's shoes, imagine what he or she is feeling, what they're doing, and then incorporate it into your scene. Don't be afraid to throw that imaginary dress," she says, winking at Courtney.

Again, my stomach turns.

"Now we have about an hour left here before the custodians kick us out. So I've broken you into pairs so you can practice a little today before heading home. When I call your names, I want each group to come up, grab your packets, and then find a quiet spot backstage or in this front hall. I'll be floating around if anyone has any questions or needs help. And remember to read your packets as soon as you get home. Inside you'll find information on audition times and locations, as well as all those dates I was telling you about earlier. Sound good?"

The crowd yells back that it is.

"All right, then, let the fun begin!"

I bring my nails to my mouth as Miss Tabitha starts calling names. It's a habit I worked hard to kick years ago, but with everything that's happened today, I decide to give myself permission for one minor relapse. With only a handful of kids left, I still haven't heard my name. That's what I get for registering so late, I think, with a frown.

And then I hear it.

"Jasmine Wilson and Ava Cantor," Miss Tabitha says.

Ava? Shoot. Again I bring my thumb to my mouth, but the nail is too short. There's nothing left to chew.

By the time I reach the stage, Ava is there, packet in hand. I grab mine from Miss Tabitha and thank her for squeezing me in at the last minute.

"Of course, we are so happy to have you," she says. "And don't worry. You're in good hands with Ava. She'll show you the ropes."

"Great," I say, forcing a smile.

Ava leads me to a quiet hall between the auditorium and girls' locker room.

"No one should bother us here," she says. "It's my favorite spot to practice. Something about the high ceilings, I swear this hall has the best acoustics."

Again, I smile although I'm not exactly sure what she's talking about.

"First time in drama club?" she asks as I fumble with my packet.

I nod. "I just signed up today. Kind of a last-minute decision."

"Well, you made a good one. Drama club is the best. Miss Tabitha is so fun, and the kids are really nice. You're going to love it."

"I hope so," I say, "though I've never exactly acted

before. I mean, what you did up there before, well, it was amazing. I don't think I could do half as good a job . . ."

Ava smiles, her eyes shifting from side to side. "Thanks, though I bet you could. It's just practice. My mom started me acting when I was just four years old. Started going down to New York for auditions and stuff. So yeah, I've had a lot of time learning on the job."

"Is it true you were on Broadway?"

She laughs. "I had a part in the Connecticut Junior Acting Academy's production of *Annie* last year, but it definitely wasn't Broadway. It was at the Shubert. In New Haven." Ava brings her hand to her cheek. "I swear, sometimes it seems middle school is just one big game of Telephone. By the time a story makes its way through the halls, it's completely different from the original. Though I gotta say, I do dream of making it to Broadway one day. I mean, can you imagine?"

"No—I still can't imagine being on *this* stage," I say.

She smiles. "That'll pass. Practice, remember?"

"Right," I say.

"I mean, you may not get to be Cinderella this time, but I guarantee if you want it badly enough, you could work hard all spring and summer and fall and next year you'd have a real shot."

"Maybe. But only because *you'd* be in high school," I say.

Ava blushes. "Actually next year I'll be in eighth grade."

"Really? Me too. I thought you were so much older!" I can feel my cheeks grow red as she shakes her head. "Guess we have opposite schedules," I say.

"Guess so," she says, turning back to the packet. "Okay, you want to give this scene a try? I'll read for the prince and you can read for Cinderella."

I swallow hard as the reality of why I'm here comes flooding back. As nice as Ava seems, she can't spare me from the harsh fact that in just a little more than a week, I'm going to have to stand in front of Miss Tabitha and read this scene.

"Uh, sure," I say. The paper shakes in my hands as I look down at the words. "Let me just read through it once first."

Ava nods, and for a moment we stand there in silence as I read the script. The scene is only a page long and the sentences are short, much shorter than I'm used to seeing in a book. But the scene requires more than just speaking. It's the one where Cinderella is trying to say good night to the prince. Where she trips and loses her slipper. And I can't help but feel a little like Cinderella, completely out of place and nervous and just wanting to get back home. But I can't run away, so instead I bring the paper up to my chin and start reading.

"Wait, what time is it?" I say.

"It's almost midnight," says Ava.

"Oh, I really have to go."

"Already?"

"Yes, I'm sorry, goodbye," I say, trying to sound panicked. I turn away from Ava and make like I'm going to run.

"Wait, but I don't even know your name," she says.

"Yes, I'm sorry, goodbye," I say again. "Oops, no shoot. I mean, 'I really have to go'—wait, no, no, that's not it . . . hang on a sec, I think I've lost my place . . ."

Dizzy with nerves, I turn to look over my shoulder at Ava, not sure whether to keep acting out the scene or to stop and find my place. And as I turn, my left ankle turns with me while my foot stays planted straight ahead.

"Ow!" I yell as I fall to the ground, my ankle twisting

while my legs hit the floor, my forehead skimming the metal lockers flanking the sides of the hall.

"Oh my goodness, are you okay?" asks Ava.

"Uh, yeah, I think so," I say. My head is spinning and my ankle throbbing, but worst of all is my heart, which is beating so fast it feels like it's going to jump right out of my chest.

Ava gives me her hand and helps pull me up.

"You need ice? We can sneak into the cafeteria through a door backstage."

I look down at the welt forming under my skinny jeans. "Maybe."

"All right, hang tight."

Ava returns a moment later with ice and a dish towel.

"At least you didn't break a leg," she says.

"Yeah, I guess so."

She laughs. "No seriously. It's not just a saying. It happened to one of my friends last year during this production of *A Christmas Carol*. She slipped on a pile of soap flakes on stage. Fractured her fibula," she says.

"Really?"

Ava nods. "See, by comparison you're doing great."

"Hah. I'm not sure I'm coordinated enough for this theater thing," I say.

Ava smiles. "Don't worry, you'll get it."

Again I nod, wondering how on earth this girl is really a seventh grader like me.

"Well, I think I'm all practiced out today."

She bites down on her lip, then nods. "Yeah, sure. No worries."

"I'm sorry we didn't get to your turn."

"Just get home safe, okay?"

I nod.

"See you at auditions?"

"Yeah, maybe," I say, then start the long hobble home, all the time wondering how I'm going to get out of this club without going back. By the time I reach my front steps, my argument is ready. I'll lead with the false advertising—the failure to mention auditions was a malicious omission—and end with my brutal fall. Only before I can get any words out, Mom's there at the door. With Dad. And Abuela. All three are fighting to hear about how it feels to be on the road to becoming a star.

For the first time in recent memory, I'm in the family spotlight. Usually that honor goes to the twins, whose sports accomplishments are much easier to get excited about. Even though I know my parents are proud when I get an A on a paper or finish sewing another bag, I've never been the one to dominate the dinner table with tales of making the winning basket or hitting a game-changing home run. And really, I've always been okay with it. But tonight, I'm surprised to find that it feels really good to see my family eager to hear from *me*. So I decide not to tell them the whole truth about the meeting. I remember Kiara talking about basketball tryouts and how awesome she said they were, even though, thinking about it now, I'm sure not every minute was as fun as she made it out to be. And so I spin my own dramatic story of running through the scene with Ava—and of how it went great.

"Oh I just knew you were gonna love it," says Mom, clapping her hands.

"Thanks," I say, hoping she can't see through my lie.

When she leans in for a hug, I realize my secret is safe.

The whole family—Mom, Dad, Abuela, Michael, Edwin and me—sits down to a big dinner celebrating my bravery. And for the first time since Kiara made those mean comments, I let myself really relax. I find myself laughing as I lean back in my seat, enjoying Abuela's stories about Mom's dancing, and Dad's talk about the first time he tried out for baseball. By the time I retreat to my room, the drama meeting is a distant memory.

That is, until I sign on to FriendChat and see I have a new message and friend request. From Ava Cantor.

U get home ok? Saw u were walking. Hope ur feeling better!! it says.

Just seeing her smiling profile picture makes my palms sweat. Ava is a star, and contrary to what I just told my family, I am most definitely not. Overtaken with embarrassment, I close out the message. *I'll write back later,* I tell myself. And instead I start thinking again about telling Mom I've made a mistake and really should just stick to starting my Etsy shop. But when she cracks open my door to say good night, her eyes still dancing with pride, my mouth goes dry. *How can I tell her what really happened after lying to everyone at dinner?* Feeling sick, I force a smile. Getting out of this now is going to be much harder than anticipated.

Chapter Eight
MYSTERY SOLVED

I slam my locker shut as my stomach fills with dread. It's the first day back from break, and I'm about to go to science, where I'll definitely have to see Kiara.

"I'm telling you, there's nothing to worry about. You and Kiara are old news," Lori says, reassuring me for the tenth time since lunch. "The only ones people are talking about now are Mary Beth and Beatrice."

"Because of Tommy Raine?"

Lori rolls her eyes. "Yes! Because of him. According to sources, their fight was epic. Mary Beth was yelling that she liked him first, then Beatrice stormed out saying he liked *her*. It was bad. And *public*. Believe me, no one cares at all about you anymore."

"Well, thank you," I say. "At least I won't have to worry about everyone staring in science class."

"Not at all," she says. "Enjoy your return to anonymity. Oh and don't forget. Winter concert. Friday, February 23. Mark your calendar!"

I nod as we part ways. Though as relieved as I am to no longer be the talk of Kiara's friends, the thought of science class still makes me feel sick. Not wanting to get there early, I add an extra loop down the hall to pass by where I first saw the mystery boy. I've done this a few times now, but so far he hasn't reappeared. This time is no different.

I continue to scan the hall until I see Ava up ahead. Shoot. I never answered her message. Embarrassed, I turn hoping to avoid her, but it's too late. She's already calling my name.

"Jasmine, hey! Great to see you're all right," she says. "I sent you a message the other night, but wasn't sure you got it."

"Oh yeah, thanks. Sorry. I did see it, and I meant to write back but then I was out all Sunday until late . . ." I say, feeling my cheeks get even hotter.

But Ava doesn't seem to notice. "It's okay. I figured

something like that happened. So how's your audition prep going?"

Audition prep? I shudder. I haven't done a thing since Saturday. Not that I can tell this to her. "It's fine."

"Oh, great. Glad to hear it. Well, I guess I'll see you later then . . ."

"Yeah, see you Wednesday." Yet as I turn to leave, I realize that if I'm too scared to quit drama club, I probably should be nicer to the star. So far I haven't exactly been friendly, even though she really has been. So breathing in deep, I turn back to Ava.

"Hey, actually, I was wondering if you had any tips," I say. "You know, things I should be practicing. Or like, songs that might be good . . ."

Ava's face brightens. "Yeah, sure. I'd be happy to help." She brings her hand to her chin. "Hmmm. You know, actually, if you aren't busy today after school, I'm having a couple people over to practice. You, uh, wanna come?"

I open my mouth, unsure of what to say. I was hoping just to start a conversation, not wrap myself into another practice session. But before I can think of how to say no, I see Kiara rounding the corner with Aliyah on her left and Carter on her right. She's eyeing me, brow raised. I pretend not to see her and turn back to Ava.

"Oh that'd be great," I say. "Thanks."

"Sure. It'll be fun. My mom's picking us up at the front entrance at three. That work?"

"Perfect," I say, then shuffle into class, which isn't as bad as expected. Turns out Noah actually enjoys dissecting earthworms almost as much as sports trivia. Which is a good thing, because before I know it, I'm in the front lobby waiting for Ava and her friends. Courtney finds me first, waving me over.

"Ava told me you were coming," she says. "I'm so glad you're doing drama—you're gonna love it!"

I laugh. "Did she also tell you I wiped out on Saturday? I'm not exactly sure I'm drama club material."

Courtney lowers her voice. "Tell you the truth, I'm not sure I am either. But that's not the only reason I'm in the club . . ."

I begin to protest her comment as she shushes me.

"Be quiet. They're coming."

"Who?" I ask, but Courtney doesn't answer.

Just then two guys saunter up, stopping in front of us.

And I gasp.

One of them is Mystery Boy.

I try not to hyperventilate as Courtney carries the conversation.

"So you're really not coming today?" she says to the other guy, her eyes following his as he leans back on his heels.

"Wish I could. Orthodontist appointment," he says.

"Yeah, way to leave me stranded," says Mystery Boy. He punches his friend's shoulder, then looks up, his eyes meeting mine. "Guess it's just me and the ladies today."

They both laugh.

"Oh guys, this is Jasmine," says Courtney. "Jasmine, this is Henry and Joseph."

"Nice to meet you, Jasmine," says Joseph, his eyes still fixed to mine.

It takes me a moment to answer. "You too," I say.

My heart kicks into overdrive, leaving me hot and dizzy. Joseph. He's named Joseph. Ava's friend. And he's in drama club! After all my FriendChat searches, all my detours through the science hall, here he is. Ready to practice for the play. With me.

Oh geez. The play. I hope he's not as good an actor as Ava—that would be way too intimidating. I try to ignore the thoughts of my clumsy fall and tell myself, *Focus. Act normal. Breathe.*

Up close, Joseph is tall and lean with broad shoulders. He's wearing the same tattered hat, though this time I see it's a Yankees cap, not gray but faded blue. He has it pulled down over his dark curls, which spill out over the sides. His skin is just a little darker than mine, more like how I look at the end of the summer. But still what makes me stop is the same thing that hooked me a month ago in the hall. Those eyes. That icy blue. They're so bright and sparkling it's hard to look away. That is until he smiles, showing off his straight white teeth. My pulse quickens as I look back at Courtney, who seems to have the same stupid smile plastered on her face as the one I'm wearing on mine.

"They're pretty awesome, aren't they?" Joseph says, grinning at Henry.

"I can only hope to be as lucky as you," says Henry.

Um, what? Were they reading my thoughts? I raise my brow at Courtney.

"Joseph got his braces off over winter break," she says. "Show off! Mine don't come off for six more months yet."

"Well, I still have no end in sight," says Henry.

"What about you, Jasmine? Ever have braces?" Henry asks.

I shake my head.

"Lucky girl," says Joseph.

I manage a small laugh but keep my lips closed, afraid he'll notice my tiny overbite, the small chip on my bottom incisor, and the crowded bottom teeth my dentist once called "borderline" for braces. Which, of course, in Mom's mind, meant they were unnecessary. Not that I ever minded until now. How could I have known back then that one day I'd be standing here next to mystery-boy-Joseph, his perfectly aligned teeth smiling down at my crooked ones? For a moment, I wish I'd pushed Mom harder for those braces.

Before I can obsess any longer, Ava comes bounding down the hall.

"Ready, guys?" she asks.

"Definitely," says Courtney.

"All right then, my mom should be right outside. Sure you can't join us, Henry?"

He shakes his head. "I'll catch you next time. You know, once I score the lead."

Ava rolls her eyes, then leads us to a big burgundy SUV. After introducing myself to her mom, I volunteer to take a seat in the third row. As soon as I sit down, I realize I'm too far back to hear the conversation, so instead I focus on my breathing as the town buzzes by outside my window. Joseph. Finally. I have a name!

A familiar ache fills my stomach as I text Ava's address to Mom so she can pick me up later. Because who I really want to be texting is Kiara. Asking her for advice on what to say, how to act. Asking her how she started talking to Carter. But, of course, talking to Kiara is not an option. So instead I stare straight out at the rolling hills and patches of forest as Mrs. Cantor drives us out farther into the countryside of Southfield.

Ava lives a few miles north of downtown and my neighborhood. From the conversation I can hear, it seems Joseph lives this way too. Well, I guess that's why I didn't know them in elementary school. Southfield isn't a huge town, but it is big enough to have ten different elementary schools which don't get mixed until middle school. After sixth grade, I thought I'd met everyone in my class. Turns out I was wrong. And this time, I'm glad I was.

Once we're at Ava's, she leads us down to her basement. Her house is much larger than mine, and while it looks old from the outside, inside it feels new. The walls are painted in soft blues and whites, and the kitchen has shiny appliances. The basement, which has yellow walls, feels more like home. There are two big leather couches, an old television, and a fridge shoved in the corner. Across from the TV, the walls are covered in framed program covers from Broadway shows.

Ava smiles as she catches me eyeing the room.

"My parents let me do the decorating down here," she says, moving toward the fridge. "Anyone want a Coke?"

We all nod back as Ava leans in and grabs four. After passing them around, we collapse onto the couches.

Ava takes a sip, then leans back, stretching out her arms. "So who wants to go first?" she asks. "And what do you guys want to work on? Songs or the scene?"

"I definitely can use some scene work," says Courtney. "I'm just gonna use a song from choir for the singing part, and I can practice that at home anyway."

Ava nods. "Jas, any preference?"

"Huh? Oh, no, whatever's fine with me. I mean, this is all so new, I probably need practice with everything."

"Don't worry. That's why we're here," says Ava.

"First time in theater?" Joseph asks me.

Too scared to speak, I nod.

"Thought so. Didn't think I remembered you from last year."

A nervous laugh sneaks out as I try to act calm. "Nope. Never done any acting," I say.

"Oh, but you can sing," says Courtney. "I remember from choir last year."

"Yeah, that's right. Sixth-grade choir. That was fun. I'm not sure I'm very good at it though," I say, my cheeks burning.

"So why drama then?" asks Ava.

I sigh, wondering the same thing.

"Well," I say, "I've always been into fashion design, like sewing and designing purses and stuff. But this winter I decided I wanted to take a break, so my mom forced me to sign up for something different. I'm not really into sports, so I thought I'd give this a try."

I look away, worried I've said too much.

But everyone just smiles. Including Joseph.

"Fashion design! That's right. I remember last year in Spanish you and Kiara used to always be talking about those classes with Ms. Chloe," says Courtney. "That always sounded so fun. You make anything you're wearing?"

I shake my head. "Nothing today. But, uh, I did make my bag," I say. I'm unsure if I should be bringing attention to it, given my experience with Kiara's friends, but I've always hated lying. So, looking away, I point to my messenger bag slumped in the corner and hold my breath.

Right away, Courtney gasps. Balling my fists, I cringe.

"You made that?" asks Courtney.

I nod. "Yeah, I mean, I dunno if it's my best work or anything but . . ."

"No way!" She walks over and picks it up. "This is awesome! It totally looks like you got it at one of those boutiques downtown. And I love the colors. Ava, check this out!"

"Uh, thanks," I say, "You really like it?"

She nods, walking the bag over to Ava. "Awesome, right?"

"Yeah, totally!" says Ava.

"You should be designing costumes," says Joseph.

I look up and for a moment I freeze.

"Uh, maybe one day," I say. "I think for now though I need a break. I love the designing part, but all that sewing. It can be tiring."

He nods.

And then we get to work. My eyes stay on Courtney as she and Joseph start running through the scene. The way she's laughing, the way her feet are bouncing, is it possible she's into Joseph too? My stomach twists when I consider the thought. As if reading my mind, Ava eyes me from the side. She motions with her hand, asking me to follow. I get up off the couch as she saunters toward the stairs.

"Be right back guys," she says. "Gonna get some snacks."

Grabbing my hand, Ava drags me to the pantry. She hands me a bag of chips.

"Doritos okay?"

"Yeah, sure," I say.

"Great. Now spill. Joseph. He's cute, right?"

"Huh. No! I mean, I guess he's all right . . ." I look away, embarrassed. Was I really staring? Are my feelings that obvious? And how can I talk about them with a girl I hardly know? I mean, if Kiara said stuff behind my back, how do I know Ava won't too?

But Ava just laughs. "All right? Come on, we both know he's gorgeous. Now usually I wouldn't bring it up, but it just turns out he's single and without a crush. And when I saw you looking at him . . . well, I thought you'd want to know."

"Uh, thanks," I say. "But how do you know?"

"He's my neighbor. We're BFFBs."

"BFFBs?"

"Best friends from birth."

"So he's your Kiara," I say under my breath.

"What was that?"

"Oh nothing," I say. "I was just thinking. I used to have a friend like that too."

Ava nods, but doesn't pry.

"But anyway, what about Courtney?" I ask.

"What about her?"

"She and Joseph. They seem pretty close."

"Oh yeah, they're good friends too. We all went to

elementary school together. Ended up in the same class for like three years straight."

"But does she like him? Because if she does . . ."

Ava laughs. "Oh, not at all. Courtney and I love Joseph, don't get me wrong, but not in that way. I mean, there was this one month last year where Courtney thought for a minute that she might have a tiny crush on him, but that was when we were doing *Beauty and the Beast* and she and Joseph had this one scene where they had to hold hands. . . . Anyway, it was all short lived. Especially now that she's so into Henry. Of course, Henry's so into Henry that he hasn't even seemed to notice, but that's a different story. So yeah. No worrying about Courtney. Or me, if that's what you're gonna ask next. Right now I'm married to the theater," she says, bringing her hands to her heart.

I smile back, but part of me can't relax. The only person I've ever talked guys with is Kiara. Confiding in Ava feels weird.

"You won't say anything, will you? I mean, even though he's your BFFB and everything?"

She shakes her head. "Of course not. Joseph's great, but I wouldn't want him getting a big head. Now, let's go practice."

"Thanks," I say, still feeling off balance. "Just, uh, maybe today I should pass on any practicing with Joseph."

"Oh, no way!" Ava says, laughing. "That'll give you away. Now come on, let's get back before Courtney starts whining for a critique."

Back downstairs, Courtney is ready for an audience. She runs through the scene twice before Ava tells her to work on her eye contact and calm down her arm movements. Then I practice a few times with Joseph—looking down at the ground almost the whole time—and once with Ava. During the times with Joseph, all I feel is sick as I struggle to read the lines, but on the last try with Ava, I actually get through the one-page scene without messing up a single word. Success! My head swells with pride as Ava raises her hand for a high five. I slap it back, letting out a whoop as I do.

"See! I told you, you could do it!" she says.

"Thanks," I say, breaking into a grin. "Now let's just hope I do it next week for the judges."

"You'll be fine," she says, and I can't help but laugh. Fine, yes. But the odds of me getting any part with an actual line are slim.

Not that this seems to matter to Courtney or Ava or even Joseph. When it's time to go, the three act like I'm just like them. And as I plop down into the worn leather seat of Mom's Honda, still humming the notes of the show tune they convinced me to sing for the audition—apparently it's one of Miss Tabitha's favorites—I realize that the lie I told about loving drama club is starting to come true. Because right now, the last thing I'm thinking about is quitting. I smile as I think of how good it feels to be tangled up in someone else's inside jokes. To sink down into someone else's old basement sofa. And to be staring straight ahead into those bright blue eyes. *Now all I need is to figure out a way to actually talk to him*, I think, turning up the radio. But first things first. I need to survive my audition. Which all of a sudden seems like the easier of the two hurdles standing before me.

Chapter Nine
CENTER STAGE

"You sure you have everything you need?" Mom asks as I grab my backpack. "Your lunch? Your water bottle? Those forms I signed?"

"Yeah, got it," I say, heading for the door.

"You sure you don't want to take some tea? I can throw some in a thermos . . ."

"No, Mom, I'm good."

"I read somewhere that tea is soothing for the voice . . ."

"Yeah, well, maybe next time. Don't want to be late!" I'm at the door now, one foot already outside.

"Shoot. I should be giving you a ride! Why didn't I think of it earlier? The cold could hurt your voice!

You know, why don't I do that? Lemme go run in and check with Abuela, see if she can watch the boys." Mom's brow tightens, and I can tell she's playing over her morning in her head, moving around all the puzzle pieces she'd have to shuffle if she were to hit Pause to take me to school.

"No, that's all right. I want to walk," I say, trying not to picture the warm car. "And besides, auditions aren't 'til after school. I'll be plenty warm by then."

Mom breathes in deep. I can tell she's relieved. "All right then. *Te quiero*. And good luck. Call me as soon as it's over!"

I nod, then start running down the frozen flagstone steps, hopping over the remnants of last night's dusting of snow. The January air feels sharp against my cheeks, and part of me wishes I'd taken Mom up on her offer. But then with my mind unable to focus on anything but auditions this afternoon, maybe the walking will do me good. Breathing in the cold, I stare at each house as I pass by, noting who still has Christmas lights up and who's already decorated for spring. A couple of houses have hung wreaths with red hearts for Valentine's Day. One still has a pumpkin displayed on its porch. From afar I can see it's been painted red, and I wonder if it's become a joke now, to see if this pumpkin can survive the seasons.

When I reach the corner of my road and Ridgeway, I pause, same as I've been doing every day for the past month. It's out of habit, really—it's not like I'm still expecting to see Kiara waiting. But every time I see the corner empty, I still sigh.

Since my first practice at Ava's house, I've hung out with her and her friends twice. One of those times I got to see Joseph again, and a part of me is still dying to tell Kiara about it. But of course I don't. Just like I don't look her way anymore during lunch. Which is actually much easier now since this week Ava and Courtney asked Lori and Cameron and me to combine lunch tables with them and some other girls they have classes with. So far, everybody's been getting along—Lori's crush sheet has proved to be the perfect icebreaker—and with so many girls at our table, it seems there's always something to laugh about. But that doesn't mean I've forgotten about Kiara and what she did. Talking about my bag and our friendship was bad enough. But covering her crime with a story about me being jealous? That's almost impossible to forgive.

The school day drags on as the knot in my stomach grows with each passing hour. Yet somehow I survive not only a pop quiz in English but an entire class of Noah talking about his upcoming snowboarding trip. After suffering through talk of ollies and nollies and other snowboard terms I've never heard before, I'm actually relieved when it's time to head up to the high school auditorium for auditions.

I use the walk to text good luck to Ava and Courtney. We all have different audition times based on last names, so the odds of running into them are small. In some ways, this is a relief. As nice as it'd be to have someone to talk to beforehand, it'd be hard to face them if I messed up, which, despite all my practicing, is still a very real possibility. I sigh, wishing I had just a few more days to go over my scene. The singing part is scary, but having done choir as a kid, learning the song has come more easily. But saying all those lines while gesturing and walking on stage? That part is trickier. And I'm still not as ready as I could be.

My heart pounds as the high school comes into view, and my phone buzzes with good luck messages back from Ava and Courtney. But their cheery words do little to calm my nerves. Hands shaking, I stuff my phone into my bag just as I reach the entrance. There's no more time to practice and no more time to worry. *It's show time*, I think, as I push open the heavy glass door.

Inside, I'm greeted with a parade of signs guiding me to a nearby classroom filled with a small group of kids pretending to focus on homework as they wait for their audition times. I sign in with the supervising teacher, then pull out my English book, but before I can even find my page, Miss Tabitha is there in the doorway, calling for me.

"Jasmine Wilson? You're up!" she says.

My nerves sizzle as I stand and try to breathe deeply. Miss Tabitha leads me onto the stage and motions for me to stand next to a piece of tape right under a spotlight. Then she walks over and sits down by the two other judges, both of whom are staring at me. *Yeah, I am so not ready for this*, I think, as my stomach flips. I fight the urge to bolt as Miss Tabitha flashes me a smile.

"Welcome, Jasmine," she says, leaning back in her chair. "We're so happy to have you here. Whenever you're ready, feel free to start singing. After your song, we'll run through our sample scene, and then you'll be done!"

"Okay, yeah. Sounds great," I say, still shaking. "I'm going to be singing 'My Favorite Things' from *The Sound of Music*."

Miss Tabitha smiles. Silently, I thank Ava for helping me choose the song.

And then I begin.

"Raindrops on roses and whiskers on kittens. Bright copper kettles and warm woolen mittens . . ."

I find the words flow out of me, the melody sounding as sweet and rosy as the lyrics. By the time I reach the second verse, I'm swaying as I sing, my arms moving from side to side as if I were a dancer. I try to look straight ahead and not at the judges, just as Ava told me, but a few times I peek back at Miss Tabitha. Each time I look, she's still leaning back, smiling. And even though I'm pretty sure she probably smiles for everyone, her enthusiasm fuels mine as I belt out the last verse. As I end the final note, I find that I'm smiling too. Ava was right. Being on stage is scary and exciting and exhilarating all wrapped up together. But most of all, being up there singing was fun.

"Thank you, Jasmine, that was great," says Miss Tabitha. "I always love that song. Or anything from *The Sound of Music*."

I smile, wondering if she suspects I had help with the song selection.

"You ready for the scene?"

I nod. "Yeah, I'm ready."

"Okay, great. I'll be reading the part of Prince Charming. Feel free to start when you're ready."

So then I take a breath, cross my fingers, and start. And find halfway through that I haven't made a single mistake. I'm getting all the lines right! I relax as I let myself slip into the part.

"Wait, what time is it?" I say, as Cinderella. The scene is almost over.

"It's almost midnight," says Miss Tabitha.

"Oh, I really have to go." I start walking toward the side of the stage, wringing my hands and pacing, and in that moment I'm not Jasmine Wilson auditioning for the school play, but a girl upset to be leaving her crush. Who, in my head, looks a lot like Joseph.

"Already?" says Miss Tabitha.

"Yes, I'm, I'm sorry, goodbye," I say.

"Wait, but I don't even know your name."

"Yes, I'm sorry, I really have to go—but thank you. Tonight, it was . . . it was . . . magical and lovely, and—"

I pause and look up as Miss Tabitha acts out the ringing of a clock. "Oh I'm so sorry, I must go . . ."

I run off stage like Cinderella fleeing from the ball, the final lines flowing out on autopilot. And before I can even think about what I'm saying or doing, I'm backstage. It's over. I did it! Without a single flub! Sure, I might not have been as emotional as Ava, and I didn't add in any fancy hand gestures like Courtney would, but in this moment, none of that matters. I remembered the lines and said them clearly. All without falling down.

"Thank you, Jasmine," Miss Tabitha says as I walk back on stage to bow. "Great job today. Remember, Friday afternoon after the last bell we'll be posting roles outside the middle school cafeteria. I will be there too in case you have any questions."

"Thank you, Miss Tabitha," I say. Then I skip off the stage and into the street toward home, my phone already out to text Mom and my new friends the good news.

Thursday is less of a blur than Wednesday, but with Ava and Courtney rehashing their auditions every time I see them, it goes by faster than expected.

Before I know it, I'm walking into the cafeteria on Friday, less than two hours away from the list posting. Ava catches up with me before I reach our table.

"What's up?" I ask, as she comes up to my side.

"Nothing," she says. "Just nervous. About the list."

I smile. "Oh, you don't need to be nervous! I'm sure you did much better than you think."

"Thanks," she says, wringing her hands. "But like I said before, I don't think it was my best performance. I still wish I didn't change my song last minute. It was definitely a little too high for me to sing well. Overall I think I did okay, though . . ."

"Though what? Even if it wasn't your best, the teachers know you. And they know you're awesome!"

"But what if they don't care? What if all they can remember is that I missed a couple high notes on that song? What if my audition just wasn't good enough for the lead?"

Ava's nerves are flying like sparks as I move my hand to her back in the hopes of putting some of them out. "Well, then you'll do great with whatever part you get. And right now I'm still thinking you're gonna be our Cinderella."

"Really?"

"Of course! When I saw you do that practice scene during that first meeting, I was blown away. You're incredible!"

"Thanks," she says. "I dunno why I'm so worried about this. I know it doesn't matter either way. I guess after last summer and having that part in *Annie*, everyone just expects me to get the lead. Usually I don't think about it too much, but today every time I run into someone they ask me if I think I'll get Cinderella. And the truth is, I don't know." She frowns. "Sometimes it's just easier to be the underdog than the favorite."

"Yeah, I know what you mean. No one expects anything from me!"

"Oh no, I didn't mean it like that."

I laugh. "Don't worry, I'm not offended. I'm still just proud of myself for auditioning. It doesn't matter what part I get."

"That's how I felt about the Acting Academy. And then I got this big part."

"Because you're awesome."

"Or got lucky."

"It's not because of luck," I say. "It's practice. Remember?"

"Hah. Yes. You're right. Okay. Now let's go have lunch. No more talk about auditions. Promise."

Though as soon as we reach our table, Courtney starts talking all about her audition. Which gets Ava going all over again about hers. And on and on they go until Lori pulls out her crush sheet.

"Guys! Big news! It turns out Tommy Raine doesn't like Beatrice *or* Mary Beth. He actually has a crush on Harper Walker!" she says, eyes sparkling.

And hearing her enthusiasm, we all laugh. Talk of auditions ceases as Lori fills us in on the latest gossip she heard during homeroom.

Before I know it, the bell's ringing and it's time for English.

"Meet at my locker after school?" Courtney says to Ava and me. "So we can all find out together?"

"Sure," I say.

"Yeah, I'll tell the boys to come too," says Ava.

My stomach flips at the thought of seeing Joseph.

"Oh, and Jas, one more thing," says Ava, as the rest of the girls disappear into the hall.

"Yeah?"

"I was talking to Joseph yesterday . . . and he was asking about you."

I stop moving.

"What? About me? What did he say? How did you not tell me this earlier!" I ball my hands into fists as my muscles start twitching.

Ava laughs. "Well, it wasn't a huge thing and I didn't want to risk having you end up on the crush sheet. But anyway, he wanted to know if we were friends before drama. You know, how we met and everything."

"And what did you tell him?"

She shrugs. "That we met at the kickoff meeting and hit it off."

I smile, still so grateful she felt that way when I couldn't see past my nerves.

"So what do you think it means?" I ask.

She shrugs again. "Not sure. Though if nothing else, we know he was thinking about you!"

"Yeah, guess so," I say. "I never know what to say to him, though."

"Yeah, I'm no good at the guy thing either," Ava says. "But Joseph's easy. Just be yourself."

I nod. That's probably good advice. But, I wonder, exactly which self do I want to be?

Chapter Ten
SWEET SUCCESS

For the rest of the day, I find myself obsessing over Joseph. Maybe he likes me. Maybe he doesn't know how to talk to me either. If only I knew what to ask him about. But what do girls talk about with guys? Their families? School? Sports? Before I can decide on a topic, I'm standing in front of Courtney, who's leaning against her locker, her hands balled together. Seeing her nervous smile snaps me back to reality.

"The list!" I say.

"I know!" says Courtney.

"I'm almost too scared to look," says Joseph from behind. From his tone I know he's trying to be funny, but his eyes look nervous.

Ava joins us a minute later with Henry.

"Guess it's now or never," Courtney says.

The list turns out to be two sheets of yellow paper taped up to the glass wall in front of the cafeteria, surrounded by a crowd of students. As we make our way to the front, I hear some cheers and sighs of relief, along with a few whimpers and "oh wells."

Ava finds her name first. "OhmiGod!" she screams, then stops, bringing her hand to her mouth. "I got it!" she mouths to us. "Cinderella!"

"Yes! I knew you would," I say.

Courtney gives her a hug before scooting in next.

"Guess who's gonna be your evil stepmother?" she says.

"You didn't?" says Ava.

"Yes! I did!"

"OhmiGod congrats! That's the other lead! I can't believe we did it. We took both the leads!"

As they embrace again, I turn to the second sheet, my eyes scanning for the Ws. After a moment I find my name near the bottom.

Jasmine Wilson—Dove, it says.

"Huh. I guess I'm a dove," I say.

Ava turns to me. "That's awesome! You got a real part—not just the ensemble! On your first try!"

I smile as the news sinks in. "Oh my goodness you're right. I'm the dove!"

"That's not a nothing part either," says Courtney. "There's a lot of singing involved. See, told ya you have a good voice."

I blush as Ava looks back at Henry and Joseph.

"How'd you guys make out?" she asks.

Joseph speaks first, his face all smiles. "King Maximilian."

"And I'm Prince Charming," says Henry.

At this, we all laugh.

"Wow, it looks like we really cleaned up," says Ava. "We took, like, all the best parts!"

"We need to celebrate," says Courtney.

"Let's go downtown," says Joseph. "Maybe ice cream? Or something warmer?"

"How about Dolce?" I say, then stop. Do I really want to go back there without Kiara? Before I can suggest something else, I hear the group agreeing.

"Oh I love Dolce, they have the best hot chocolate!" says Ava.

"Yeah and they make this white chocolate one too," says Courtney.

"And don't forget the salted caramel," says Joseph. "I get it every time."

I bring my hand to my mouth as we grab our bags and slip out the front doors, wondering how many times Joseph has stared up at the Dolce chalkboard and ordered a salted caramel steamer, never even knowing the two girls who created it. For a moment I debate telling him the drink's history, but by the time I'm back in the conversation, the moment has passed. Joseph is talking like King Maximilian, chasing Henry down the sidewalk. Ava's on the phone with her mom, Courtney's head is buried in a text. I decide to do the same, writing to Mom that I scored a small part. And then I savor the moment, smiling wide as we follow the road under the highway, over a creek, and then back under the train tracks before reaching downtown.

When we arrive, Dolce is empty, giving me little time to think about my order. I let the others go first, my heart pounding as Joseph orders the salted caramel steamer. But I decide not to follow suit. Today is about new friends and new adventures. So I order the mocha mixer and a chocolate chip cookie instead. The girl behind the counter, a high schooler who's been working this shift for years, does a double take but doesn't question me. I'm grateful. There are parts of Dolce that will always be just for me and Kiara. That drink is one of them.

Though it turns out the mocha mixer isn't too bad. I down it in minutes, amazed by how a drink can sweeten my mood. Everyone is still talking about the play, discussing Monday's first song practice—we need to learn the music before we can start learning lines—and analyzing who got which part. Henry was smart enough to snap a picture of the whole list, and we go through it part by part, talking about how it's going to be the best performance yet.

"The Kapoor sisters won the other animal roles," says Ava, turning to me. "They're both great singers, and really sweet too. You'll love hanging out with them."

"Oh cool," I say, still a little unsure how this whole rehearsal thing works. "Will I just be with them, or will I see you guys too?"

"Don't worry, we're all gonna see each other until we're sick of it," says Henry. "You'll just hang out with the people in your scenes the most."

"Usually they break us into groups for rehearsing and stuff," says Joseph. "But that won't be for a few weeks yet. Once we finish with the songs."

"Right. Songs first."

He nods, and I can feel my face burning as I try to think of what to say next. Joseph is right there across the table, looking at me and leaning back in his lime green metal seat. But nothing comes to me. It's like my brain decides to shut down every time his bright eyes shine into mine.

Luckily, Ava saves me. "So, enough with the play. Anything fun going on this weekend?" she asks.

Joseph shakes his head. "Catching up on some video games?"

"Yes! I am way behind on War Tales," says Henry.

Courtney laughs. "Seriously? You guys are gonna celebrate with video games?"

"What? It's, like, two degrees out. And with rehearsals starting, who knows when I'll have another free weekend," says Joseph.

"True," says Ava. "Though I was thinking more along the lines of a movie. I saw that Crushed is playing at the theater downtown."

"Oh, I've wanted to see that," says Courtney. "It looks super cute."

"Ugh. Total chick flick," says Henry.

Courtney sticks out her tongue. "Well, if you go, I'm totally in," she says to Ava.

"Great, let's do it!"

And then for a moment, everyone stops talking. I know that this is when I should invite myself along, to say that I've been dying to see *Crushed* too. Only I've been knocked off balance by a wave of sadness, my mind all tangled up in thoughts of Kiara and me and Dolce, planning our own weekend adventures. As great as it feels hanging out with Ava and Courtney, it's just not the same.

"So Jas, are you free? Any interest in *Crushed*?" asks Ava, her voice unsure.

And it's then that I realize I've been frowning, staring at the door.

I blink once, then smile. "Oh yeah, that'd be great! I'd love to," I say.

"Good. Let's text tomorrow," says Ava." We can figure out a time to meet then."

The weekend planned, we all part ways. Once I'm

alone, thoughts of Kiara come flooding back. As I pass by our old corner meeting spot, I can't shake the feeling that my current happiness would be sweeter if I could share it with my old best friend.

When I open my front door, I'm surprised to find streamers overhead and my entire family buzzing in the kitchen.

"Congratulations Jazzy!" says Mom, running over to give me a kiss. "I couldn't be prouder!"

I drop my bag by the front door before following her into the kitchen. "Thanks, Mom. Is all of this for me?"

"Of course," she says. "Getting a part in your first play is such a big deal! It deserves a celebration."

And then for the next two hours Kiara is the farthest thing from my mind as I eat, laugh, and talk with my family. Mom has made my favorites tonight—empanadas, arepas and fried plantains, served with a side of Dad's special French fries and gravy—and I dig in, devouring a huge plateful. About halfway through the meal, Michael and Edwin start a game of Pictionary, drawing animal shapes in their gravy, and holding up their plates for all to see. At first Mom rolls her eyes and asks them to stop, since gravy spills off their plates every time they lift them up, but then Dad starts shouting answers, and soon we're all laughing and playing along.

"Lion—no, jaguar—no, cheetah! No, no it's a . . . oh I don't know, it's a jungle cat!" Dad yells as Michael draws.

"No, it's a fox!" says Mom. "Definitely a fox!"

"*Lobo! Lobo, lobo!*" yells Abuela, baring her teeth like a wolf.

Michael shakes his head before editing his picture, a glob of gravy hitting me in the chin as he adds stripes to the animal's torso.

"Horse!" says Mom. "That's a horse!"

Another shake.

"Zebra!" I yell. "The stripes! It's a zebra!"

Michael nods, then grabs my hand and raises it with his. "We have a winner!"

"Woo!" yells Edwin.

"I still think it looks like a cat," says Dad.

We all laugh.

"All right, all right," says Mom. "It's time for the coconut pudding!"

She throws two towels at Michael and Edwin, who get to work sopping up the gravy. We dig in to dessert, and I'm reminded that this celebration is for me. And that, unlike dinner after that first drama club meeting, this time I've earned it. It feels good and overwhelming all at once to think of the many new things I've done in just one month—and of all the new possibilities still lying ahead.

Chapter Eleven
LUNCH BUNCH

"So, oh my God, did you see how cute Henry looked yesterday?" says Courtney between bites of popcorn.

Ava rolls her eyes. "Girl, Henry might be nice to look at, but he's totally wrapped up in Henry. Ugh. The last thing that boy needed was to win the lead."

"I know, I know," Courtney says. "But seriously, I don't care. I mean, he's funny and cute and totally stuck in my head. So he's a tiny bit into himself? It's a speed bump, not a road block."

Ava shakes her head. "I think you've gone crazy."

Courtney giggles. "Hey! That's not fair. Henry *is* nice . . . sometimes. And he's super funny in class. And I mean, he's going to make such an adorable

Prince Charming . . ." She drops her voice to a whisper as the lights dim and the previews fill the screen. "And it's not like I'm the only one with a crush." She gives me a nudge and a smile.

"Hey! What's that supposed to mean?" I say. I can feel my heart start thumping.

Courtney looks at Ava.

"Don't blame me, I didn't say a word! She figured it out herself," says Ava.

"But there's nothing to figure out," I say.

"Right," says Courtney.

Ava pats my back. "No worries, Court's not a gossiper."

"Obviously," says Courtney. "You think I'd say anything about you with all you know about Henry? Geez, can you imagine if he ever found out how much I talk about him?"

Even in the dim theater, I can see her cheeks turn red.

"I think he'd see it as a compliment," I say, and they both laugh just as the opening credits of *Crushed* fill the screen.

After the movie, we decide to go to Dolce while we wait for our moms to pick us up. But it's closed, so we end up at the ice cream shop next door instead.

"So how tough are these rehearsals gonna be?" I ask after Courtney finishes comparing Henry's hotness to that of the main guy in *Crushed*.

Ava smiles. "Finally! A conversation where I can add value," she says. "The next few weeks should be pretty easy as we work on the songs. I mean, don't get me wrong, there will a lot of hard work, especially for you practicing your solo and stuff."

"Solo!" I blurt, my eyes wide. I didn't quite realize a solo would be involved in the part of the dove.

Ava shoots me a smile. "Don't worry, Jas. You're going to do great! Miss Tabitha is always so nice in rehearsals. She's not intimidating at all. After songs, we practice the scenes, and then the last week, with dress rehearsals, gets pretty crazy. And then we have the performances. They're definitely the best part."

"I can't wait," I say, trying to stay optimistic and ignore the lump forming in my throat related to my surprise solo. *Miss Tabitha is sweet, and she'll go easy on me*, I tell myself. I cling to this thought until Mom picks me up.

Back home in my room, Ava texts good night, and I replay the evening in my head. I really do have new friends! Despite Courtney's quizzing me on Joseph, I had a fun time tonight.

As rehearsals for the play begin, my nervousness quickly turns into excitement. The next few weeks pass just as Ava described. We focus first on singing the ensemble songs before breaking into groups to work on smaller scenes. I get to know the other girls playing the animals, Ana and Samira Kapoor. They're both excellent singers, and very sweet, just as Ava described. We practice our scenes during each rehearsal, and sing the song with my solo so many times that by the end of each rehearsal, the words all jumble together in my head. After a few weeks, we start calling ourselves "the animal squad," and then others catch on too, calling us "the squad" for short. It feels good to be a part of the squad, and I smile every time I hear someone say it.

In addition to all the rehearsals, I run through my singing and speaking parts in the evenings for Mom and Abuela, and sometimes even during lunch with Ava and Courtney. Three weeks into rehearsals, Henry and Joseph join us, squeezing two extra chairs between Courtney and Ava at our already-crowded lunch table. This causes quite a bit of whispering among the other girls—none of us has ever sat at a lunch table with boys before!

Having Joseph at our table is an extra challenge for me when we start running through our lines. I can feel Lori's eyes on me as I sneak a peek at Joseph during my turn and then miss a word, my cheeks growing hot. *Can she tell I have a crush on him?* I worry about it all through lunch—I don't want my name to be added to her crush sheet. Luckily, she doesn't seem to notice.

Ava smirks at both me and Courtney as we leave the cafeteria. "Girls, you need to get it together, or Lori is going to have a field day!" she says.

"I know, I know," I say, blushing.

Courtney giggles. "Sorry. We were unprepared. Having them at our table is just so . . . *public*. But next time we'll do better. We'll be very professional."

Ava rolls her eyes. "Okay . . ."

But Courtney is right—each day they're at the lunch table is more comfortable. I get very good at saying hello when Joseph shows up, and even find myself laughing with him when we bring almost the same lunch from home. And while I never muster up the courage to have an actual conversation with Joseph, I find that as the days pass, I'm more relaxed about having him sitting across from me. And all the practice really does help with my lines.

Which is a relief, given that the play is now only two weeks away.

"You did great today," says Ava as we grab our bags and head out to the high school lobby to wait for our rides home. It's February now, and the cold has made walking home almost unbearable, especially as rehearsals are now dipping from afternoon into evenings. Though according to Ava, the next two weeks are when things get serious. This week we're adding a special Saturday rehearsal. Then next Monday we start dress rehearsals. Then Friday, March 9, is opening night. It's all a little overwhelming, yet exciting too. After all our hard work, I'm eager to see everything come together.

"Yeah, you were awesome," says Joseph coming up from behind.

I feel myself tense as he smiles at me, his eyes meeting mine.

"I—uh, thanks," I say.

"Of course. Anyway, I'll see you later. That car's mine," he says, pointing at the latest set of headlights.

As soon as he leaves, I breathe. "Geez, when's it gonna get easier? Talking to Joseph's harder than singing in the play!"

Ava laughs. "We seriously have to work on this. Seeing the two of you just smiling at lunch and tip-toeing around rehearsals is *killing* me," she says. "He obviously likes you, and you like him. Like, all you have to do is talk to each other!"

"I know, I know. But I can't. Every time he's around, my brain just malfunctions."

"Well, I guess I know what we'll be doing at Friday's sleepover then," says Courtney, joining us.

"And what's that?" I say.

"Practice!" they both shout.

"More play practice?" I say innocently.

Ava rolls her eyes. "No! You know exactly what we'll be practicing."

"All right, all right," I say, just as Mom pulls up. "So you still up for the concert beforehand?"

Both girls nod and I smile back. I'm happy they agreed to go to Lori and Cam's band concert when they asked us last week, and even happier to be having a sleepover. I haven't had one since my last sleepover with Kiara, and that was months ago. Having one with my new friends makes me feel like I've really moved on.

"So I'll see you tomorrow then," I say, reaching for the door. Ava stops me before I can exit.

"You know, Joseph's little sister is in the band," she says. "He might be there too. Should I ask him to sit with us?"

My stomach swirls. "I . . . uh, I'm not sure," I say. Having him across the table at lunch is one thing, but sitting with him at a concert feels almost like a date. Especially since Lori only asked the girls.

Ava smiles. "Why don't I just ask him? It might be weirder if he sees us there and no one mentions it."

Still unsure, I nod. "Okay, unless . . ."

"Unless what?"

"Well, I don't want him thinking I'm stalking him or anything . . ."

"Don't worry, Jas," she says. "I'll just tell him the truth. That we're going to hear Lori and Cameron play and I remembered his little sis. Trust me, it'll be fine."

"Well, keep me posted then."

"I'll text you after I talk to him," she says with a wave.

For the next twenty-four hours, she leaves me waiting for that text. At lunch, the boys don't show—they still spend some days sitting at their old table—and when I ask Ava about it she just shrugs.

"Don't worry, he'll write back," she says.

But I do worry. All day long. Every class feels twice as long, and every muscle feels tense as my mind keeps circling back to Joseph.

I chat with Lori on our way out of English. "So, I'm excited for the concert tomorrow," I say as we pour into the hall.

Lori smiles. "Me too! We've been working so hard, it's really gonna be an awesome show!"

"I can't wait to hear you guys," I say as we reach the spot where we part ways. "You're both gonna be great!"

"Hope so," she says and for a moment I linger, wondering if she'll say anything else. I've been waiting to see if she'd fill me in on any other gossip about Kiara, but for the past month, there's been nothing about it from Lori, even when we've been alone. Too much time spent on the crush sheet, I figure, and I head down the hall to science.

As I shuffle in just ahead of the bell, I'm not surprised to see Kiara's seat still empty. She's been out all week, and I can't help but feel jealous, wondering where her parents have taken her on vacation this time. Every February her dad goes somewhere cool on business and Kiara and her mom tag along. Last year, it was Australia. The year before that, Spain. With her luck, she's probably somewhere warm and tropical this time, like Hawaii.

Oh well, I think, blinking away visions of palm trees. She can have Hawaii. I have the play. And a fun night tomorrow. Which may include Joseph! I feel for my phone, stuffed into my jeans pocket, willing it to buzz with a text. Even though I know Ava wouldn't send one during school, I can't help but wish.

She makes me wait another four hours until I'm in my room at my desk, trying to figure out a math problem set that seemed way clearer in class.

He's in! it says.

I grip my desk as if holding on to the side of a tipping boat. I'm tingling. Excited and scared and oh my gosh, so nervous.

Not knowing what to say, I send a smiley face back.

Don't worry, it'll be great, she says.

My phone buzzes again as I'm typing *Fingers crossed.* And before I know it, I see my text has gone not to Ava but to Kiara.

Kiara?

My hands are full-on shaking now. I blink at the screen.

Yes. Kiara has just texted me. One word.

Hey.

And by mistake I've texted her back. Meaning she knows I'm on my phone.

I hold the phone like a hot potato, part of me wanting to fling it across the room, the other part wanting to call Ava for advice. But I haven't told her much about Kiara, and the thought of telling her the whole story now exhausts me.

Kiara's text is probably a mistake, anyway—it was probably meant for Beatrice or Aliyah. Breathing in, I send my response before I can talk myself out of it.

Sorry! Meant that for someone else prob like u did too! Ttyl!

As soon as I send it, another message comes back from Ava. We exchange a few more before saying good night. Yet sleep does not come easily. Because every few minutes, I'm looking down at my phone. Only the message I'm waiting for never comes.

Kiara doesn't text back.

Leaving me to wonder why. Was it really a mistake? Or did she want something from me?

I grapple with the "what ifs" until my eyes burn with exhaustion. Around midnight, I find I can no longer keep them open. *Her text must've been a mistake*, I tell myself once and for all. Then I let my mind drift away, and close my eyes tight.

Chapter Twelve
MUSICAL CHAIRS

The auditorium is buzzing as Ava, Courtney, and I enter to find seats for the band concert. "Will it really be this full for the play?" I ask.

"Even more. Standing room only!" Courtney says.

I swallow. "Really?"

Ava nods. "They usually sell out every performance. But don't worry. You really can't tell from the stage."

"Right," I say. Her words do little to calm my nerves, which have kicked into overdrive ever since we walked into the high school. As if the day wasn't stressful enough, wondering about Kiara and worrying about Joseph. At least Kiara still wasn't back in school. Now that I'm at the concert, there's no avoiding Joseph. In fact, he'll be here any minute. He told Ava to save him a seat. And of course Ava thinks he should sit on the end, next to me. As much as I'd like that, I am still not sure I'm ready to be that close. I mean, I'm just starting to get the hang of saying hi at lunch. Could I really sit next to him for two hours—in the dark? Better to have a buffer. And who better than Ava, his BFFB? Which is why I think I should sit farther in. Courtney agrees, just as long as she's close enough to watch whatever happens.

Ava leads us down to the main aisle before we can decide. "Well, we better sit before the seats are all gone. Oh look, down there. Looks like four right on the end."

As we walk, I position myself between Ava and Courtney, hoping we'll file into the row in the same order. But Ava stops us when we reach the empty row.

"Go in last," she says.

I shake my head. "I don't think I can."

"Come on, it'll be fine. It's a show. It's not like there's much talking."

"I know, but still. Please. I'm too nervous. Just take the end."

She sighs. "Fine. But you better sit next to me. Courtney, you go in first."

"Hey! But then I won't hear anything!"

Ava raises her brow.

"Okay, okay," she says.

In silence, we shuffle in. Courtney, me, and Ava. We leave one seat empty at the end.

Though as soon as we sit down, Ava's popping up again.

"Hey, be right back!" she says.

I turn to Courtney. "Where's she going?"

She shrugs. "Maybe to find Joseph?"

My heart beats faster, picking up more speed when it turns out Courtney's right.

"Hey ladies," she says, Joseph in tow.

She hangs back and pushes him into the row first, leaving him sandwiched right between me and her.

I hold my breath as my stomach rolls into a somersault.

"Hey Jas," he says with that picture-perfect smile.

"Uh, hey," I say, trying to ignore the pounding in my chest.

He smiles back at me again, and I do the same.

And then we sit there. In silence.

I can tell Ava's eyes are rolling without even looking.

"So, Joseph, when is your sister on?" Ava says, saving me. "She still playing the trumpet?"

He nods. "I think sixth grade is on right after intermission. And then she's got a solo in the finale. She's getting really good."

Courtney leans so far over, she's almost in my lap. "Oh wow, that's so cool. You'll have to point her out to us," she says. Looking at me, she asks, "Lori and Cameron both play clarinet, right?"

"Uh, yeah," I say. "I mean, Lori does. Cameron plays trumpet."

Joseph's eyes light up. "Oh cool. I wonder if she knows my sister."

"M-maybe," I say.

Just then the lights dim, saving me from any further conversation. Joseph leans back in his chair and I do the same, hoping I look calm and relaxed even though my insides feel like someone just lit off a case of fireworks. And then for the next forty minutes, I make myself stare at the stage and not at Joseph. I don't let my eyes meet his, even when I think they're looking my way. Instead, I force myself to look for

Lori and Cameron. To count the number of overhead lights. And it works. By the time the first half ends, I'm feeling more relaxed. And grateful I decided to wear a sweater. I'm pretty sure the shirt underneath is drenched in sweat.

As the curtain closes for intermission, Joseph turns to me. "Hey guys, anyone hungry? Court? Jas? Ava? Want me to grab anything at the snack bar?" he asks.

Courtney and Ava both nod.

"I'd love a cupcake from the bake sale," Courtney says.

"And I'll take popcorn," says Ava.

They both reach for their wallets. Then Courtney stands up. "Sorry, but I need the bathroom."

"Me too. Go together?" says Ava.

"Yeah, we'll be back," Courtney says, sliding by me.

And before I know it, I'm sitting there alone with Joseph.

"Hey, wanna come with me?" he asks. "I could use an extra pair of hands."

"Uh, yeah. Sure," I say.

"Great, follow me," he says, leading me into the crowd.

I follow him, still in shock from Ava and Courtney's disappearing trick.

"You enjoying the show?" he asks as we file into line.

"Yeah. Definitely," I say.

And then there it is again. Silence. As kids and parents mingle and smile and swirl around us, neither of us has anything to say.

Come on, Jas, say something, I think.

And, mustering up every ounce of courage, I do.

"I'm, uh, I'm excited to hear your sister though. That's so cool she plays trumpet."

Joseph smiles, and I wonder if he's as relieved as I am that I've thought of something to say. "Yeah, we're a pretty musical family I guess. My older sis is really into theater, like me."

"Oh nice," I say.

Before I can say more, someone taps me from behind.

Still jittery with nerves, I whip my head around fast.

And find myself face to face with Kiara.

"Jasmine! There you are! I've been looking all over," she says, all smiles.

"I—uh, what?"

I turn to Joseph as the world begins to spin.

"Hey, I was wondering if we could talk," says Kiara. "I was away all week and so much happened, and well, I know the timing's not ideal, but—"

"No," I say before she can finish. "I can't talk. I don't *want* to talk."

The words come out sharp and loud. I can tell the people near us are listening. That I'm making a scene in public. Yet as Kiara asks me again, I find myself yelling even louder.

"I'm sorry," I say. "But I'm busy. I can't talk to you right now."

"Please?" she asks, her eyes now thick with tears.

I shake my head. She reaches for my hand. "Hey, Jas, I know. I know I've been awful. But please? I just got home tonight, and your mom said you were here and after your text last night I just thought it'd be better if I could see you, you know, in person."

Tears well as I shake my head again. "No, I'm sorry. Please. Just leave me alone."

Kiara's face falls. "Fine. Be that way," she says, then disappears into the crowd.

Now the whole line is staring at me. I watch as

hands are brought to mouths, whispers passed between friends, phones grabbed and texts sent. What have I done? I need to run far, far away. To crawl into a hole. And never come out.

My head spins like a carnival ride as I turn to run. And trip over my feet. I wobble forward, then fall. Right into Joseph.

He helps me up.

Oh geez. How can I ever talk to Joseph now?

"Hey Jas, you okay?" he asks.

"Yeah, I'm, uh, fine," I say. "I, I just need to . . . I just need to go."

Joseph frowns. "Hey, it's all right. Just calm down," he says. "Stay with me. Watch the rest of the concert. My sister hasn't even gone on yet."

I nod, but I know I can't stay. The tears are already flooding my eyes. My nose is running like a faucet.

"I'm—I'm sorry," I say, "but I'm really not feeling well. I think I need to go home."

"You sure? Hey, why don't I get Ava or Courtney?" he says.

Shoot. Ava and Courtney. Our sleepover. Why does Kiara have to ruin everything? For a minute I contemplate staying. Wiping my eyes and standing strong, just like Kiara would do. But I've never been good at hiding how I feel, and seeing Kiara has opened up a wound I don't think I can deal with in public. So I shake my head.

Joseph sighs. "Who was that girl, anyway?"

"She's just—just an old friend," I say. "But I do think it'd be better if I just go home."

"All right. Let me at least walk you out."

I nod, too dazed to say any more.

"Let me know when you're back safe, okay?" he says.

"Yeah, sure," I say. "And, uh, tell your sister congrats from me."

He shoots me a weak smile before leaving me by the door.

Once I'm alone, I run. For once, I don't notice the cold.

Chapter Thirteen
WE NEED TO TALK

I wake up Saturday morning with twenty-seven missed texts and a pounding headache. Four are from Ava, three from Courtney, and two from Joseph. The remaining eighteen are from Kiara.

The lump in my throat returns before I even get out of bed.

I groan, rubbing my forehead. All I can think about is the crowd staring at me. The missed sleepover. And of how Joseph looked at me when I ran away. Will he ever talk to me again? Will Ava? Or Courtney?

Hands shaking, I decide to read through my messages. But before I can start, my phone rings.

It's Kiara.

I hit Ignore.

But then it buzzes. A new text floods my screen.

Please, it says. *I'm walking your way. I NEED to talk.*

And as the lump grows bigger, I throw on some clothes. Joseph and Ava and Courtney will have to wait. I can't ignore Kiara any longer.

I run out of my house before Kiara can ring the bell and meet her on the street.

"So. What do you want?" I say, crossing my arms.

Kiara's eyes are red, her hair messy and wild.

She opens her mouth to speak, yet nothing comes out.

A moment later, I hear a whisper.

"I'm sorry," she says.

I frown, wondering what this sorry means. Is she sorry she tracked me down at the concert and embarrassed me in front of Joseph? For bailing on JKDesigns? Or for what she said back in November? Most likely she's thinking only of last night, I think, given how long she's avoided me. I wait for a moment to see if she'll say more, but nothing comes. Suddenly, I feel a rush of anger. What is she doing? Now that I have new friends, she wants to come mess that up for me, too?

"You're not forgiven," I say. "I don't even know why you're here, *face friend.*"

Her face crumbles into her hands as I spit my words.

"I know, I know, I've been so awful," she says.

And as she cries, I step forward, the anger growing with each step. Like a steaming tea pot, I'm boiling over, unable to hold in my feelings any longer.

"Awful doesn't even start," I say. "I mean, what you said about me to your new friends was awful. But then to blame it on *me*? To tell everyone that it was *my fault* we stopped hanging out? That I was *jealous*? I mean, come on, Kiara. I listened to your basketball stories, went to your games and cheered you on, tried to hang out with you and your new friends—even when you had no time for me or JKDesigns or anything I care about. I tried, Kiara, and you threw our friendship away like a piece of trash. So forgive me if I don't feel like talking to you. If I'm maybe still a little angry about how you've acted for the past few months, including— make that *especially*—last night."

Her mouth falls as she stares back at me. After a minute, she nods her head.

"I know," she says. "You're right. I never meant for everything to get so out of hand."

"If you didn't like my bags or want to do JKDesigns, you could've just told me," I say.

Kiara looks down. "I know. But Jas, the thing is I *do* like your bags. Actually, I love them!" I give her a look of disbelief, but she goes on. "If anything, *I* was always a little jealous, of how the design thing came so naturally to you. Part of why I tried out for basketball was because I wanted to find something I could be good at, like you are at fashion design."

"But you're good at it too! And that still doesn't explain what you did to me."

She sighs. "So I can make a hair clip, big deal. It's not like designing a bag or an outfit."

"You know I still can't make a dress pattern."

"But one day you will, and then you'll go off and be famous without me."

I look at her, baffled. "So because you're afraid I'm better at fashion design, you thought it was a good idea to make fun of me?"

She shakes her head. "No, that's not it! I just wanted to be good at basketball, and part of that was getting those girls to like me! Only, all they care about is talking about boys and making fun of other girls. So when they started making fun of you . . . well, I knew it was wrong, but I went along with it. I knew they wouldn't be my friends if I didn't."

I stare at her, stone-faced.

She sighs. "Aliyah started the rumor that you were jealous. When you ran away in the hall, she called you a jealous crybaby. The story kind of grew from there. And even though I knew it wasn't true, part of me wanted to believe it. To blame you instead of myself."

"We were best friends, Kiara. Didn't that mean anything?"

"I never meant for you to hear," she says.

"So? That doesn't make it any better," I say. "And then you knew that I did hear . . ."

She looks up, then down and away. For a moment she is silent. Then she whispers. "I chose them."

I try not to cry as the pain comes flooding back. "So why are you here now? They're your chosen friends."

She frowns. "They're not exactly my friends. At least not Aliyah or Mary Beth. Turns out your bag isn't the only thing they hated. I heard them making fun of my headbands too."

"Surprise, surprise," I say. "And here I thought they were giving you tons of orders."

She sighs. "I know. I told you, I messed up. I thought if I could act like them, then I could *be* one of them. But really, they were just laughing behind my back. All their help getting me together with Carter? It was just so Mary Beth could get closer to his best friend. At least Beatrice is nicer. Having her has kept me sane. But deep down, it's still been tough. I still miss my best friend."

"Right. Who's that, again?" I say, even though I know what she means. Plenty of times I've wished Ava and Courtney knew me as well as Kiara did, and that they could read my moods or get my jokes or understand what I mean without me having to explain. But just because I miss what we had doesn't mean I'm ready to forgive her now.

Kiara reaches into her pocket for a tissue. "I'm sorry, Jas. I should've apologized months ago. But then this stuff started happening at home and it's been so upsetting. I'm just so scared. And you're the only one I trust."

Stuff happening at home? I guess that's the reason Kiara's here. But would she have ever tracked me down if this problem never came up? I'm not sure how to respond.

"Look, Kiara," I say. "I'm not going to lie. I can't just make the past few months go away. But . . . it's pretty clear you wouldn't be here if you didn't need me. And you were my best friend for almost my whole life. So why don't you come in, and we can talk."

"Oh Jas. Thank you," she says, still teary. "But your house? With your mom and dad and Abuela?" Again she covers her eyes. "I don't think I can face them. Can we walk? The beach?"

I cringe. As much as I love the beach, in the winter it's twice as cold and the wind gusts twice as strong. But I can tell from Kiara's face that she really needs me to say yes. So I nod.

"Sure. The beach. Let's go."

Kiara looks up, her eyes meeting mine. "Really?"

"Yeah. Now start moving before I change my mind."

We walk in silence through our neighborhood and across Main Street, where we begin the half-mile trek down Ocean Road. The road is flat and traffic is non-existent this time of year, so we walk down the center of the street, avoiding the sidewalks made slushy by the night's snow now melting in the afternoon sun. Down by the dunes, we head to the boardwalk and follow it to the sand. There's no snow here, the air just warm enough to keep it from sticking.

Kiara walks over to an empty lifeguard tower and starts climbing. I rub my arms then follow. Once we're both seated, she sighs.

"You're not too cold?"

I shake my head, ignoring the breeze. "So what's up?"

She frowns. "I don't know where to start."

"How about at the beginning?" I say.

And as she raises her puffy eyes to mine, she doesn't look like the same girl who made fun of me in the halls. She seems smaller. Younger. More like the girl who I used to have sleepovers with every week. Who'd grab my hand when we crossed the street, and who'd talk all the way to Ms. Chloe's as we dreamed about JKDesigns. The past hits me like a punch to the stomach, even though I'm still steaming mad. I nod, encouraging her to continue.

"Well . . . it's my dad," she says. "He . . . he lost his job."

"What? How? He's like the smartest guy I know."

She shrugs. "Downsizing, whatever that means."

"Well, don't worry, I'm sure he'll find another soon."

"But that's the thing," she says. "This happened in December, and he still hasn't found anything. If he doesn't find something soon, we're selling the house and moving. Next month."

"Wait. Moving? Next month?"

She nods.

"Where?"

"Georgia," she says, her voice flat. "To live with my grandma."

"Whoa," I say. "Is this why you weren't in school last week?"

"Yeah," she says. "We went to Savannah to visit Grams and check out the middle school. I spent a day there, following around some student ambassador like a lost puppy. The school was so much bigger than here, and the kids all had these different accents. Every time I talked, someone would laugh and ask where I was from. It was so uncomfortable."

"But I thought you loved Savannah," I say, thinking back to her annual summer trips.

"For vacation," she says, "not life."

"But can your dad can find work there?"

She nods. "His brother, my uncle, works at some aerospace company. They need engineers. He got my dad an interview. We find out next week if he gets the job."

She rubs down her arms as a breeze whips by us.

"Let's start walking. It'll warm us up," I say.

Kiara nods and we climb down from the chair.

"Well, that'd be great if he can get a job," I say.

"Great? I have to pick up and leave all my friends and everything I know, and you think it's great?"

"Well, no. I see why you're upset. But I think there are a lot of cool parts of this too. Like getting to meet new people and live somewhere warm. It's a new adventure."

"Yeah, one where I have to live with my grandma."

I shrug. "I'm sure that wouldn't be forever."

She sighs. "I know. Honestly, I just don't know what to make about any of this right now. There's one job he's waiting on here, but if that doesn't come through, Mom and Dad say we're moving no matter what. They said we don't have the money to stay here much longer, and at least at Grams's we won't have to worry about paying the bills. But it's all just so up in the air. Who knows where we could end up, Jas? Not to mention that everything I know is here. They're talking about moving in three weeks! I won't even get to finish my first basketball season!"

Kiara is crying now, her cheeks slick with tears.

My eyes fill as I try to stare out to the distance, focusing on the horizon, where the sky meets the outline of Long Island. I try to visualize the choppy water lapping up on that opposite shore. Is the beach empty, or if we could zoom in would we see a couple of kids huddled under their coats, talking just like us? I blink, trying to fight through the wave of emotion sitting like a lump in my chest. Poor Kiara. All the time I was picturing her in Hawaii. All those times I looked down when she passed by, when I saw her laughing with her new friends. Smiling at Carter in class. I thought she was happy and everything in her life was perfect without me. All that time she was living with this secret that she might have to leave.

For a moment, I don't know what to say. It's easy to keep saying things will be fine, but it's impossible to know if they will.

"Leaving would be really hard and scary," I say.

"But I still think that if it happens, it could turn out to be okay. I mean, just a couple months ago you didn't know Beatrice at all, and then you joined the basketball team and now you're like BFFs. Who's to say the same thing can't happen in Savannah?"

"I guess . . ." she says.

"And look at me. Abuela moved in with us like a year ago now, and sure, it was a little crazy at first getting used to all her diabetes medications and excessive video chatting, but overall it's been a good thing. Really nice actually. She's taught me how to cook and helped with my sewing, and I haven't had to spend as much time babysitting the twins," I say. "So living with your grandma, I mean, maybe that could be good too."

"Maybe," she says.

"And just think about the weather. It'll be warm!"

She smiles, then sobs again. "Oh Jas, thank you. I don't deserve this, you talking to me, especially after the scene I caused last night."

"You definitely don't," I say, my mind jumping back to Joseph.

"I know. God, I'm so embarrassed. But you don't

know what a relief it is to talk to you. How good it feels. So many times I wanted to tell Beatrice or some of the other girls, but I just couldn't, you know?"

I sigh. "Yeah, I do."

And then as our walk deposits us back at the road where we entered, Kiara extends her hand.

"Tick tock?" she says.

And even though I have no idea where we're headed, and I'm still not sure I can forgive her, I say the words back.

"Tick tock."

Chapter Fourteen
COSTUME CATASTROPHE

By the time I get home, I have ten more messages from Ava and Joseph in addition to those I still haven't read from earlier. There's also one from Lori. I deal with the easiest first.

Congrats, Lori, u guys were awesome last nite!! Sorry I had to leave early—tell Cam I say congrats too!!

I send the message off to Lori, then shoot off a smiley when she thanks me. Then knowing I'll have to face Ava and Joseph at our afternoon rehearsal, I begin damage control. I send Joseph a quick text thanking him for last night and saying everything's okay, then I call Ava and, after apologizing profusely for bailing on the sleepover, I give her the short version of what happened with Kiara.

"So basically she dumped you, then made a scene last night because her other friends weren't so great after all? Talk about dramatic. Maybe *she* should join drama club," Ava says.

"Hah, you're right. She'd probably be the star. But I am sorry for running off and ruining our sleepover plans. I know I shouldn't have freaked out like that, especially in front of Joseph . . ."

"Hey, don't worry, I talked to him before. No one's angry. We were just worried."

"Well, thanks. I think everything's okay now. I mean, we're def not friends again, but she shouldn't be hunting me down again anytime soon."

"Good, I'm so glad to hear things are all right. Though . . ." Ava pauses for a second, then continues. "That's not the only reason I was texting. I really hate to spring this on you with all you have going on, but it turns out we have a bit of a problem."

"Problem? With what?"

"The play." Ava sounds upset. This can't be good.

"Okay . . . what's up?"

She sighs. "It happened last night after the concert.

Turns out it was one of the sixth graders' birthday, so a few kids had a cake in the practice room after almost everyone had left. And even though everyone knows candles are strictly forbidden, I guess someone lit a few and then threw them in the trash. Only they weren't fully out and some papers in the trash can lit on fire. Or maybe they didn't really light on fire, but one of the kids *thought* they did. Anyway, everyone started yelling and someone grabbed the fire extinguisher and started spraying. And at first everyone thought this kid was a hero because he put out the fire before the smoke alarms could go off or anything. And really it shouldn't have been a big deal, except . . ."

"Except what?" I ask, heart pounding.

"Except before the concert Miss Tabitha moved our costumes in there so they wouldn't be in the way. And I guess a bunch of them are now covered in white foam from the fire extinguisher."

"Are you serious? Who told you this?"

"Joseph," she says. "His little sister was there."

"So what does that mean for us?"

She breathes into the phone. "I'm not sure. But after Joseph called, I emailed Miss Tabitha to see if

I could help out or anything. And she told me that about half of the costumes were destroyed and that we're gonna need new ones."

"What about the person who made them originally? Can they re-create them?" I ask.

"That would be Ms. Mahoney, the old literacy teacher. She made them years ago when the school first did *Cinderella*. And now she's retired and living in Florida!"

"So what happens if Miss Tabitha can't find someone to make new ones?"

"Well, her note was pretty vague, but I got the feeling that it was serious. I just hope this doesn't mean they have to cancel the play!"

I can tell Ava is starting to panic. "What? Would they do that?" I ask.

"I don't know, but what are we going to do without half the costumes? Anyway, I wondered if maybe you'd be able to help, since you've done so much sewing."

"Wait. You want me to make the costumes?"

"Well, yeah. I mean, could you?"

"I . . . I don't know," I say, taking a deep breath. "I do love to sew, but I haven't done it in a while, and . . .

full costumes? I mean, are there patterns for them? Or would I be making stuff from scratch? Because I'm not really that great at designing clothes . . . I really only know bags."

"Well . . . how different can it be, right?"

I bow my head and find myself staring at a clump of lint on the floor. It rolls around the wooden boards in perfect rhythm to the heat vent a few feet away. Back and forth. Right and left. I try to think. Sewing costumes is very different than making bags. I cringe, envisioning my failed dress pattern shoved in the back of my closet, now covered with months of dust and neglect.

"I think we need to talk to Miss Tabitha," I say. "I mean, two weeks is not much time. And rehearsals are starting to get really busy. I just don't know . . ."

"Okay," Ava says. "Well, rehearsal is in an hour, so we can talk to her then."

"Yeah. Let's just hope it's not too many costumes."

Only, once we talk to Miss Tabitha, it turns out the damage is worse than we thought. We've lost two of Cinderella's costumes, one of the stepsisters' costumes, all the animal costumes, and all the dresses for the townspeople in the ensemble! Everyone is on edge as Miss Tabitha tries to reassure us that we'll be okay.

"I know there have been a lot of rumors floating around about canceling the play. And I want you all to know that we absolutely will *not* be canceling," says Miss Tabitha, a smile plastered to her face. "After all your hard work, there will be a *Cinderella*! But this obviously will change things a bit. Since we don't have the time or money to re-create what we had, I'm asking you all to go home tonight and look in your closets. Old Halloween costumes, dresses from dance recitals. I want you to bring it all in. Together we'll go through the pile and create our own costumes!"

The room erupts into groans.

"But Miss Tabitha, we've worked so hard! Without real costumes, no one will take us seriously!" yells Courtney.

"Yeah, it'll be a mess!" says a voice from the back. "No one will match!"

"Isn't there a way to get *real* costumes?" asks Henry.

Miss Tabitha sighs. "All right everybody, now calm down. I know this is a disappointment, and I want the play to be a success just as much as you do. But remember, the play will be great because of *you*, not because of what you're wearing. So, go home tonight and see what you have. I promise, we'll make it work."

Ava turns to me. "Old Halloween costumes? Come on, you have to help," she says.

I breathe in deep. "I told you, I'm not good at designing clothes."

"But we have nobody else! And Court's right, without real costumes, the audience will be distracted. It'll be a mess!"

"Yeah, but you heard Miss Tabitha. She said we'd think of something."

"Yes! And *you* are our something!"

"I . . . I just don't know."

"Come on, Jas, we've worked too hard for this to all fall apart now!"

"Yes, but sewing costumes is so much work. I mean, maybe if I had someone who could help me . . ."

I close my eyes and think. And that's when it hits me. I already know two people who fit the bill. Ms. Chloe and Kiara.

Breathing in, I raise my hand.

"Miss Tabitha?" I say. "I actually know how to sew. And I have some friends who do too. And, uh, I'm not

sure I can make the costumes as great as the originals, but I'd love to try."

"Oh my gosh, Jasmine, really? You would be our
hero!" says Courtney.

"Yeah, Jasmine, that'd be awesome!" says Henry.

"Go Jas!" says Joseph.

And before long everyone is talking at once.

"Guys, guys, please. Order!" says Miss Tabitha.
"Now Jasmine, that is awfully sweet, but I really think
that's too much work. I can't ask that of you."

I nod, ready to agree, but then I see Ava's face. The
tears welling in her eyes. And I want to do this, for my
new friends and myself. I want the play to be great.

"You're not asking," I say. "I'm volunteering. Let
me just make a couple calls. See if I can get a few people to help."

Miss Tabitha looks relieved. "Well, if you're sure,
then go make those calls! We'll have you practice last
today. And Jasmine, if this turns out to be too much
work, tell me. We can always make do with what we
have."

I nod, then slip off stage and into the hall. I call
Ms. Chloe first. She agrees before I finish speaking.

"Of course I'll help," she says. "Anything for the

school. And an excuse to see you. I've missed you, Jasmine!"

My cheeks warm as I realize how much I've missed Ms. Chloe too.

"Really? Oh thank you, you'll be saving the play!" I say. "So, Miss Tabitha says there's a closet full of left-over fabrics and stuff here. I'll bring over what I can later this afternoon so we can get started. The deadline is tight."

"And I'm between DIY classes, so the timing couldn't be better," she says.

I end the call feeling a little surer of my plan, though no more relaxed about making the next call. But then if Kiara wants *my* help, she owes me hers. So I bite down on my lip and hit Send before I can chicken out.

"Hey," she says, her voice quiet. "Everything all right?"

"Hey, uh, yeah, sort of. But it'd be better if you could help me out . . ." And then I dive in, telling her about drama club and the costumes.

"Wait. Are you seriously in the school play?" she asks when I finish.

"Yeah."

"You auditioned and got a part?"

"Uh-huh."

"So you haven't been spending afternoons at Ms. Chloe's?"

"Not since I overheard you and your friends."

"Whoa. Who is this girl and what has she done with my old friend?"

"Same girl, new interests."

"And friends."

"Yup. New friends."

Kiara sighs into the phone. "I'm still so sorry. For everything."

"I know. And I'm still not over it."

"Yeah. Right," she says. "So anyway. You need to fix some costumes for the play and you want me to help?"

"Yes."

"All right. Um, yeah, I can do it," she says. "I mean, I don't have a ton of time with basketball, and you know that whole maybe-moving thing, but I have this weekend off. There's a tournament for the older girls, but I'm not going."

"Can you meet me at Ms. Chloe's at three?"

"Sure."

"Great," I say. "And Kiara?"

"Yeah?"

"Thanks. This will really help me out."

I run on stage between scenes, my phone still in my hand.

"We have a plan!" I say, breathless. "Ms. Chloe, who runs the local DIY club, and one of my friends are gonna help out. The costumes may not be as fancy as Ms. Mahoney's, but I think we can do something for all of them so we don't have to wear hand-me-downs!"

"Oh, Ms. Chloe! I know her—she's wonderful," says Miss Tabitha, smiling. "All right, if Ms. Chloe thinks you can do it, then I think this is the best option we've got. But you'll send me an update each day? Let me know if it's too much?"

I nod.

"Okay. Then, yes, we have a plan," she says, then yells out to the crowd. "Ana, Samira? Let's get all the animals on stage now. I want to run through this scene once before we let Jasmine go."

Ava shoots me a thumbs-up as I join the Kapoor sisters in the center of the stage. She mouths "good luck" a few minutes later as I bolt for the door.

And then after calling Mom for a ride and filling her trunk with the entire contents of Miss Tabitha's theater closet, I head to Ms. Chloe's. Kiara arrives ten minutes later, two salted caramel steamers in hand. A silent peace offering. I grab one and smile.

"Oh girls, how I've missed you," Ms. Chloe says once we're all together. "Now, let's get to work!"

We spend an hour sorting fabrics into piles and divvying up costumes. There seems to be enough leftover fabric to make everything we need—a relief, since it will save us money and time, both of which are in short supply. Ms. Chloe starts right away on Cinderella's maid outfit and agrees to make the step-sister costume as well.

"I'll take the animals," I say. The original costumes were just simple pullovers made of felt. Re-creating them seems easy.

"Oh, from what you described, those seem pretty simple," says Ms. Chloe. "Why don't I take those as well, and you focus instead on Cinderella's gown?"

Shoot. My stomach jumps as I think of all my failed pattern attempts. Of all the dresses I've made way too small with sloppy seams and uneven sleeves. And I know that this is too much. How can I make not just a dress, but *the* dress? The one Ava will wear during the climax of the show?

I shake my head as Ms. Chloe shoots me a smile.

"The gown? I don't think I can do it," I say.

"What are you talking about?" says Ms. Chloe. "You are an expert sewer. Of course you can do this!"

"Well . . . do you, uh, have a pattern I can use?"

"Check the back. I should have some basic dress patterns there. But don't let those hem you in. I've seen your sketchbook, and I think we'd all love to see a Jasmine original."

"But . . . I . . ."

Ms. Chloe walks over and places her hand on my shoulder. "Don't worry, Jasmine, I know you can do this. With your skills, there is no one better suited for the job."

I swallow. "Okay," I say.

"Okay?"

"Yeah."

"Great!"

"So isn't that everything? What am I gonna make?" Kiara asks.

"I was thinking you could help with the ensemble," I say. "There are fifteen girls who need costumes for the ball, and we have no time to make them gowns. So I thought, what if we raided the costume closet and used old dresses from different shows? I know they're all different styles and everything, but I thought maybe if you made special headpieces to go with them, we could pull it all together."

Kiara's eyes brighten. "Sure, that's a great idea. Maybe I can even use feathers and flowers so they look more old-fashioned."

"Perfect!" I say. "I think I have some silk flowers and rhinestones here too, from Miss Tabitha. I saw a bag of them around here somewhere . . ."

"Right here!" says Ms. Chloe, throwing it toward Kiara. "And I think that's a fabulous idea. Now let's get working. We've got exactly two weeks to pull this off, and today is almost over."

"We can do it," I say, thinking of all the kids depending on us. "I know we can!"

Then Miss Tabitha grabs a roll of tulle and flicks on the music. As we start working, my mind drifts. What if we can't pull this off? What if I end up disappointing everyone? Will I ever spend time with Joseph again? Or will my chance be over, before I've even figured out what to say?

Mind swirling, I follow Ms. Chloe's lead and reach for the tulle. And then I let myself get lost in the moment, my hands moving in time with the music.

Chapter Fifteen
FIRST BLUSH

As I begin sketching concepts for Cinderella's dress, Kiara plops down in the chair next to me, a pile of wire and feathers in her hands.

"So you're gonna try another pattern?" she says, eyeing my paper.

I nod. "I'm going to give it one try. But if it doesn't work, I'll just grab one of Ms. Chloe's patterns on Monday."

"Good plan," she says, turning to her wire. "Now tell me more about this drama club thing. I still can't believe you're in the school play!"

"I know, it's pretty unbelievable, huh? But after all that happened, I just needed a break from fashion.

And the first day, I met Ava and then she introduced me to her friends Courtney and Joseph and Henry and we all started hanging out. It's crazy—they're all in our grade, but besides Courtney I'd never seen any of them before."

"I don't know Ava or Courtney, but wait. Did you say Joseph?"

"Yeah."

"Joseph Cruz?"

I shrug, realizing I still don't know his last name. "I'm not sure," I say, "but I know he lives north of town."

"Yeah, that's him," says Kiara. "I know him from social studies. He's super cute. Wait, you were standing next to him at the concert last night, weren't you?"

I nod.

She frowns. "Gosh, I've been such an idiot."

"Yup."

"So then you and Joseph. What's the deal?"

I look away from Kiara. "Nothing. We're just friends."

"Oh my gosh," says Kiara, eyeing me.

"What?" I say.

"You're blushing!"

"Huh? No way," I say, still staring at my paper.

"No, you totally are. Look! Your cheeks are red."

I frown. "Must be the heat. Ms. Chloe always keeps this place like a sauna."

"Right. And it has nothing to do with you having a crush on Joseph."

"What? No! Who told you that?"

Kiara laughs, poking me in the side. "No one, silly. Well, you did, with all that blushing!"

"Cut it out!" I say, poking her back. "Joseph's a friend, nothing more."

"Well, that's great," she says. "That's the best way to start. Just keep talking to him, and before you know it, he'll be holding your hand."

"Hah. Right," I say, rolling my eyes.

"Hey, I'm serious!" Kiara says. "You're smart and funny and pretty and you know I've always been envious of your long, wavy hair . . ." Kiara runs her fingers through my curls, pulling them out when they get stuck in the ends. "Why wouldn't he like you?"

I shrug, still afraid to look in Kiara's direction. It feels weird to be here, back at Ms. Chloe's, talking with Kiara. Even weirder to be talking to her about Joseph. And to hear her call me pretty? Well, that's the strangest of all. Besides Mom, no one's ever called me that before. And it's not something I've really wasted time thinking about either. I've always felt smart—my report card is good evidence of that. And funny seems to run in the family.

But pretty?

I glance over at the mirror hanging in the corner and look. Same long, wavy hair, same big brown eyes greet me. My flat nose balancing out the full pink lips beneath it. My teeth are almost straight and besides a splattering of tiny pimples on my forehead, my skin is clear. So all right. I'm having a good skin day. And my hair does look shiny. But could I really be pretty in the way that a boy would notice? The compliment feels like a pair of baggy jeans I still need to grow into.

"Well—I mean—thanks," I say, cheeks even redder. "He does seem to like talking to me when we're together, but uh, I don't know. I just always get so nervous around him!"

"That's your problem," says Kiara. "You just need to relax. Talk to him like you would a best friend. And tease him a little. Then laugh about it. I'm telling you, guys love that stuff."

"But how?"

"Oh I don't know, I used to make fun of Carter's hat. It was so dirty and he like never washed it, so for like a month every time I saw him I'd grab it off his head and ask him when he planned on washing it . . ."

"No, not the teasing. I mean, uh, I can see how that worked for you and Carter, but I don't know if teasing is really my thing. But the talking. Like he's a best friend. How do you do *that*? Every time he's around, I freeze up!"

Kiara smiles. "It's not easy, right? Makes you feel kinda sick. But you gotta just do it, same way you just got up in front of those judges and auditioned for the play. And that took real guts, by the way. I could never do something like that."

"Sure you could," I say. "Look how easily you talked to Carter and made friends with everyone on that basketball team? I mean, you had them all wearing your headbands like you were BFFs in like two seconds."

Kiara frowns. "Maybe, but I didn't go about that in the right way, did I?"

"Maybe not. But what about Carter?"

"Yeah. We had fun hanging out, though I think that's over. We never really hit it off. Like, once we got talking, it turned out we like very different things. Besides, there's this eighth grader on the boy's team, Fernando, and geez, Jasmine, I swear. He is beautiful. And hilarious. Ever since I caught a glimpse of him, Carter just can't compare." Kiara erupts into a fit of giggles.

"Hah. I'll have to look for him in the halls. But back to Joseph. I still don't have a clue of what to say!"

"All right, all right," she says, wiping the smile off her face. "Let's get back to business. You got an extra sheet of paper?"

I pull one out from under my sketch.

"Why don't we write down some conversation starters? You know, different topics. That way next time you're hanging and Joseph's there, you won't have to waste time thinking of what to say. You'll already be prepared."

"All right, makes sense. But I still don't know what to say."

"How about we start with his family? Does he have any brothers or sisters? How old are they? Do they get along? And then, oh what about drama? How long has he been acting? Has he ever had such a big part before?"

I shrug as Kiara keeps firing questions. "I know he has two sisters. No clue about the rest."

Kiara grins. "Get writing," she says.

For the next hour, Kiara shapes wire, I sketch dresses, and every few minutes we add another conversation topic to the list. It reminds me of how we were before basketball, only somehow it feels different. It's the way Kiara talks, no longer all giggly but more sure. And then there's the way we're talking to each other. How I'm not as scared to chime in and say what I want to say. Somehow it's is easier, now that I have new friends. Not that it isn't nice to be talking again. Still conflicted, I chew on this as I sketch, thinking of how much meeting Ava and her friends has changed me. By the time I stop to take a breath, it's already seven o'clock.

"So what do you think? Should we start again in the morning?" asks Ms. Chloe.

Kiara and I both nod.

"Great, I'll drive you home," Ms. Chloe says.

And as our buckles click in her tiny SUV, all I can think about is how good it feels to be back at DIY club. And how I really hope I can come through with the costumes.

Chapter Sixteen
A Happy Surprise

"How's it going?" Kiara asks, holding up another headpiece. It's her fourth in three hours, and this one looks even better than the last. It's a big barrette, covered in tiny blue and white flowers, each with a rhinestone in the center. On each side are scrolls of metal, intertwined to look like vines.

When I see it, I gasp, then place it next to the last she finished—a headband covered in metal stars and feathers.

"They're amazing," I say.

"You started the pattern for the gown?" she asks.

I nod. "Cutting the fabric for it now."

"I'm happy to help if you need it."

"Thanks, but I probably just need to try it on Ava. Though, actually, you're about the same size as her . . ." I grab my tape measure and wrap it around her waist. "Since she's not here . . ."

"You want me to fill in?"

I nod. "Now stand still. I have some pinning to do."

Grabbing the fabric I've already cut, I bypass my empty dress form and start pinning the pieces right onto Kiara's body.

She giggles as the fabric brushes her cheeks. "Hey, that tickles!" she says.

"Shhh, I need to think," I say.

She rolls her eyes but cooperates, standing for almost an hour as I cut, pin, glance at my sketch, then adjust again. My final design for the dress is an off-the-shoulder ball gown, with little beaded sleeves that graze the elbows. The dress is fitted to the waist before flaring out in an airy skirt. It's beyond ambitious given my limited skills, time, and fabric, but on paper it looks so pretty. And I know if I can get it right, it'll look amazing on Ava.

"So, are you done? Can I look?" asks Kiara as I back away from the fabric.

I nod, then walk her over to the mirror hanging on the wall.

"What do you think?"

She laughs, glancing over the yellow fabric and pins. "I think I need to see the final product."

"Fair enough," I say, then grab her shoulders, moving a row of pins by half an inch. "There. Now I'm gonna just sketch out some lines and then you can take it off."

The sketching takes the rest of the morning, which Kiara—and my stomach—reminds me of once she's finally freed.

"We need to get some lunch," she says. "I'm starving."

"Me too. Uh, Ms. Chloe?" I ask, yelling out to the sewing machines in the back. "Should we break for lunch?"

Before she can answer, the door buzzes.

"One second," Ms. Chloe says. She flicks off her sewing machine and runs to the front. I turn back toward my pattern just as she opens the door.

"Surprise!" say Ava and Joseph, pizza boxes piled high.

"We've brought you sustenance," Joseph says, sliding them onto the table next to me.

I shake my head in disbelief. "Seriously. This is awesome."

"And this isn't even all of it," says Ava. "Court and Henry should be up in a minute. We sent them to Dolce for drinks."

"Courtney and Henry, huh?" I say, raising my brow. Ava winks.

I smile, wondering if Ava set up this alone-time herself, or if maybe now they're officially a thing. Before I can ask, they're back, carrying two trays of salted caramel steamers.

"I figured these were safe," says Courtney. "I remember everyone saying they liked them."

"Definitely," I say, grabbing one. "But how did you find us? I can't believe you're here!"

Ava drapes her arm around my back. "Just looked it up on Google. What'd you think we were gonna do? Leave you to save the play on your own?"

I laugh. "No. Well, yeah, actually. I did."

"We're here, and we want to help," says Joseph. "So put us to work."

"All right. I think I can arrange that," I say, turning to Kiara.

But she's no longer by my side. Out of the corner of my eye, I see her back by the sewing machines.

"Hey, Kiara, get over here," I say.

She frowns, then shuffles over.

"Guys, this is Kiara," I say.

"Hi guys," she says, looking down. "You, uh, might remember me from the other night at the concert. I'm, um, sorry I made kind of a scene."

For a minute, everyone is silent.

And then Joseph smiles. "Hey, no worries. You're helping us now. And we need all the help we can get. Pizza?" He points to the box.

"Uh, yeah. Sure," she says, grabbing a slice.

And then, awkward introductions over, we hum along to the radio as Ms. Chloe and I assign tasks to our new workers. We show them how to glue feathers and sequins to the old dresses we're using in the ensemble, and how to hang and steam the finished products. Once they have it down, I resume work on the dress pattern, first trying it on Ava, then pinning my pieces of yellow fabric to the fancy blue fabric. It's time to cut, the step that has me the most nervous.

Before I can start, Joseph walks over and grabs the chair next to me.

"Anything else I can help with?" he asks.

I pause for a moment to think.

"Well, I'm going to have to start sewing this soon," I say, pointing to the dress. "But after that I'm going to need to add sequins and beads. You think you can sort these into piles by size?" I ask, pointing to a jar on my right.

"Yeah sure," he says.

I smile, then start to cut, remembering Abuela's words about making things bigger, not smaller. I grab my ruler and make my final cut lines two inches bigger than the pattern. *This one* has *to fit*, I think, as I start cutting.

I work in silence, trying to focus on following my guidelines, on cutting straight, on making each piece a little larger than I've drawn. Yet every few minutes my eyes drift up to Joseph's. After a half hour, I realize his are doing the same. *Gosh, Jasmine, you need to say something*, I tell myself, but even after all of Kiara's help, nothing comes to mind.

That's when I feel a familiar tap on my shoulder.

"Hey guys, how's it going? Decided I needed a

break," says Kiara, stretching her fingers.

"It's going well," I say. "Hoping to get the bodice sewn today while Ava's here. If that fits, the skirt should be easier," I say, grateful that a flowy skirt isn't as hard to fit. "Then I can focus on the skirt and finish work this week. Joseph's getting the beads ready for me now."

She smiles. "That's awesome. I can't believe how much you've gotten done. I still have like eight more headpieces to go."

"Only eight? That's amazing!"

"Yeah, except my fingers feel like they're about to fall off."

Joseph and I laugh. And then there's silence.

Not knowing what to say next, I resume my sewing.

But Kiara doesn't leave. "So Joseph, how'd you get so into theater?" she asks. "Been doing this a long time?"

"Uh-huh," he says. "Ever since I was a kid. My older sister was into it, and I got dragged to so many rehearsals that eventually my mom thought it made sense to sign me up too. Though I haven't always been so into it. Last year, I went through this time where I really wanted to quit. Kinda like you and your sewing I guess," he says, turning to me.

"Really?" I say. "But you're so good, why would you want to stop?"

He shrugs. "I don't know. It was right before sixth grade started. All my friends were signing up for football and soccer and there I was rehearsing for another town play with my sister. It had never bothered me before, but with starting middle school and everything, I dunno, I just wanted to try something else. I was sick of being 'that theater kid' you know?"

I nod. "I do. Definitely," I say, thinking of all the lonely walks to Ms. Chloe's after Kiara started playing basketball. "So what happened? Did you end up quitting?"

"Yeah, for like a week. I didn't even tell my parents. First day of school, instead of going to theater practice, I went to soccer tryouts instead."

"I'm sure they loved that."

"Yeah, not so much. My sister covered for me the first couple days, but then on the third, practice ran over, and I didn't make it in time for pickup. They were furious."

"So did they make you quit soccer?"

He shakes his head. "Nah, turns out they didn't even care that I wanted to try something new. I spent months thinking they'd freak out, and they were like 'son, you wanna try soccer, no big deal.' But they were pretty angry about the whole lying thing."

"Of course. So what happened?"

"The next day I got cut from soccer. Turns out I'm a better actor than runner. I couldn't keep up with the sprints."

I laugh, then notice that Kiara is no longer behind me. She's back at her table, working on headpieces.

"I can't believe she . . ." I say under my breath.

"What's that?" asks Joseph.

"Huh? Oh nothing," I say. "I just can't believe you were cut. I can't imagine you having trouble with anything."

"Haha, oh believe me. There's tons of stuff I'm terrible at. Like math and swimming and buying new clothes . . ." He grabs his shirt, another faded T-shirt, and laughs. "So why'd you quit your fashion design stuff?"

My cheeks burn as I look down at my fingers, still cutting the blue fabric into pieces for the dress top. Of course I can't tell him about what happened with Kiara. So I settle on telling him the other truth, the one I didn't even know about until I got started.

"Yeah, well, I guess I was thinking it'd be good to meet some new people," I say. "I love fashion, but there aren't a lot of other kids who do it from school. And really, I think I just needed a break. Right before I quit, Kiara and I were over here every day trying to get stuff ready to start an Etsy shop. I had this idea I'd launch a shop and start selling clothes and get together this portfolio I could use for design school. But all that preparation took a lot out of us. Too much time focusing on one thing, you know?"

"Yes!" says Joseph. "I felt the same way."

"But you came back to acting."

"I did, but I also joined a few clubs."

"And you're happier?"

"Definitely."

"Me too. Turns out I really enjoy singing," I say.

"That's why you're perfect as the dove." Joseph's cheeks redden as he turns back to the beads.

"Thanks," I say, before letting the silence once again envelop us. Though this time it doesn't feel as awkward. And as I finish up my cutting, I realize that Joseph is more than blue eyes and dark curls. He also thinks a lot like me.

My mind floating, I leave Joseph and retreat to the sewing machine in the back, anxious to get the dress bodice sewn. Leaving off the sleeves, I sew from the waist up, focusing on the wide neckline and little darts that will help it fit snugly. I make the whole top a half inch bigger than I'd measured, hoping Abuela is right and that it'll be easier to take it in than be left with fabric pieces that are too small.

Right before five o'clock, just as I'm finishing the top, Ms. Chloe flashes the lights.

"Sorry guys, I have dinner plans tonight. We'll have to lock up in fifteen minutes," she says.

Everyone gets to work finishing up. I rip the almost-done bodice off the machine and pin together the last seam.

"Ava, I need you for a second," I say.

"Sure," she says, running over.

"Try this for me," I say, motioning to the bathroom.

"Oh wow, is this part of my final gown?" Her eyes twinkle as she grabs it from my hands. "This is so exciting! I'll be right back."

As the bathroom door closes, my throat goes dry and I start sweating. *Please fit, please fit, please fit*, I say over and over to myself.

And it does!

When Ava emerges, the top is not too small, but a little big! I run over and throw my arms around her.

"It fits!" I say. "Kiara, Ms. Chloe, look! The bodice! It *fits*!"

They both cheer. "I knew you could do it," says Ms. Chloe.

"Yeah, and look at it! It's gorgeous. It's gonna be way cooler than if you'd just used one of those pre-made patterns," says Kiara.

Ava turns to me. "So you did this all on your own?"

I grab my sketchbook. "Yeah, from this," I say, pointing to my drawing. "The final dress will have these little sleeves, and this beading, and then this big flowy skirt . . ."

"Whoa," Ava says, shaking her head. "You are beyond talented. And to think, they wanted me to wear an old Halloween costume. Can you imagine? This is way better!"

"Thanks," I say, my cheeks growing warm as I throw a few pins in the top. "Though, uh, let's not get ahead of ourselves. I still need to finish the dress."

"Well, you're off to a great start," Joseph says, surprising me from behind.

I smile just as Ms. Chloe claps her hands. "Sorry to break this up, but you guys ready to head home?"

"Yeah, just a minute," says Ava, running to the bathroom.

She emerges seconds later and hands me the bodice. Then I slide one of Joseph's bead piles into a plastic bag just as Ms. Chloe shoos us toward the door.

"Homework?" says Joseph, eyeing the beads.

"Oh yeah. It's gonna be a busy two weeks," I say.

"Don't worry," he says. "The fun has just begun."

Chapter Seventeen
READY OR NOT

I wake up on Monday with a jolt as the first rays of sun creep in under my shades. I roll over and stare at the clock. 6:55 a.m. Ten minutes until my alarm. I debate shutting my eyes, then think of the busy day ahead. School, rehearsal, costume making. Within seconds I'm awake, my mind ready to start the day. Which gets off to a better start than usual, especially when I find Kiara waiting in our old spot on the corner.

"Hey, good to see you," I say, waving as I get closer.

"Yeah, you too," she says, only her voice falls flat.

"Everything okay?" I ask.

She shrugs, her breathing heavy.

"Your dad?"

She nods.

I breathe in, that sick feeling returning to my stomach. So much for a good morning. I bite down on my lip as I wait for her to catch her breath. Ever since yesterday when she helped me talk to Joseph, I've thought of little else. But seeing Kiara's face brings me back to the reality of why we started talking. That our rekindled friendship might be cut short.

"So what happened?" I tap my feet against the ground as I fight the sensation to bite my nails.

After a minute, Kiara speaks.

"They called him back to Georgia. He's flying down tonight. Meeting first thing tomorrow."

"Who called him? That job?"

"Uh-huh. They emailed him this weekend. My mom told me this morning."

"So does this mean he got the job?"

She shakes her head. "Don't know. But would they really be flying him down to tell him he didn't?"

"No. Probably not."

Kiara blinks, then rubs her glassy eyes. "Sorry. The wind. Gets me every time."

"Yeah, me too," I say, my own eyes growing wet.

"Well, your parents said they'd move whether he got this job or not, right?"

"Right," she says with a sigh.

"And the only way they'd stay is if he got that other job here."

"Yeah."

"Any news on that?"

"Not yet."

"Then this is good."

"How is it good?"

"Because it doesn't change anything. If he gets the job in Georgia, then you won't have to stay with your grandma as long. What really matters is if he gets the job here. Because if he doesn't get *that*, then . . ."

Kiara bows her head. "I know you're right . . ."

"But?"

"What if he gets both jobs and he makes us go anyway? I mean, Dad's always talking about how much he misses Georgia." Kiara's voice wavers, her words a whisper.

"He wouldn't do that," I say. "This is your home. You said he lost his job like two months ago. If he wanted to move away, don't you think he would've done it then instead of hanging around here?"

"Maybe, but . . . oh I don't know. Parents are just hard to read, you know? Like, so many times I think they'll do one thing, and they do another. What makes sense to them doesn't always make sense to me."

"Tell me about it," I say, thinking of Mom waving that Parks and Rec flyer in my face over break. "But sometimes things that don't make sense in the moment make a lot of sense later. Though I still have my fingers crossed you'll stay here."

"Me too," she says, kicking a stone across the sidewalk.

"You know, you don't have to keep working on the headpieces if it's too much," I say. "I really appreciate all you did this weekend. And I know you have basketball this week."

Kiara shakes her head. "There are only five headpieces left. I can't stop now!"

"Good. I mean, great! I couldn't do this without you."

Kiara smiles. "Thank you."

"For what?"

"For, well, everything," she says. "For talking to me, even when you probably hate me. God, sometimes I hate me. Or at least how I acted. The last couple months, well, I've really missed you. A lot."

I breathe in, and for a moment I don't know what to say. I settle on the truth.

"I've really missed you too."

She smiles. "Hey, later this afternoon after practice I'm supposed to be meeting up with Beatrice at the mall. I was thinking maybe if you have time, you might like to come with us?"

Kiara tugs at her coat as Southfield Middle comes into sight.

"I'm afraid today's gonna be pretty busy with rehearsals and the costumes and stuff, but next time for sure. Okay?"

"I think I can arrange that. Maybe next time you can even invite Joseph."

"Maybe," I say, my palms growing sweaty. "Though if we're inviting Joseph we may need to do a movie."

Kiara raises a brow as we reach the entrance.

"You know, less talking?"

"Oh Jas," she says, taking my arm. "I saw you yesterday, you were great with him!"

"Yeah, and the whole time I felt like I was gonna faint!"

"Tell you what. Basketball this week is late on Tuesday and Thursday. How about we meet at Dolce after school a few times, go over a few more pointers?"

"Now that's a plan," I say, then shoot her a smile as we part ways for class.

And then for the next six hours, I try my hardest to focus on school. But every chance I get—at lunch, during study hall, when I should be reading in English—I pull Cinderella's bodice out of my bag, along with the little ziplock bag of beads.

"Welcome to March Madness," Joseph says, catching me with my needle on the side of the stage. "You ready for the final push?"

"Ready or not," I say, sewing on another bead.

"Do you, uh, need any more help this week?" he asks, his hips swaying from side to side.

"Uh, no, I think I'll be all right," I say.

He nods, then walks off to rehearse his scene. A few minutes later I run into Ava and Courtney, who are off to do the same.

"That's looking so awesome. I can't believe I get to wear it," says Ava as she passes by.

"Thanks," I say, just as Miss Tabitha motions for me backstage. I throw my sewing back into my bag and follow her out into the hall.

"So I talked to Ms. Chloe last night," Miss Tabitha says. "She said you're making great progress with the costumes. How are you feeling? You still okay? It's not too much?"

"No, uh—I mean, yeah. It's going great," I say.

"And Ms. Chloe said you should have them done in time?"

"Hopefully," I say. "She's working on most of the sewing, and one of my friends is making these head-pieces so all the girls at the ball will have costumes. And I've been working on—"

She cuts me off before I can finish. "Sounds great! Now I told Ms. Chloe it'd be great if we can have every-thing by this weekend for dress rehearsals, so we have some time to practice, but if that's too much . . ."

Her voice trails off as a lump forms in my throat. All this time I've been thinking we had two weeks, not one. But Miss Tabitha's right. We need time for everyone to practice walking and dancing in their costumes.

My stomach churns. "Um, yeah, that should be fine."

Her face brightens. "Great! I'd love to see them on Friday if possible, you know, just so we can make sure there aren't any problems before we hand them out on Saturday. Would that be all right?"

I nod even though I have no idea whether everything will be done.

"Wonderful. Now go practice your scene, and as soon as you're done, get out of here. I've thrown a lot on your plate, and I don't want you exhausted before the show starts."

"Of course," I say, hands trembling. "I won't let you down."

Chapter Eighteen
YES TO THE DRESS?

On Thursday, I track down Ava after school and make her try on the almost-finished gown. It's a little big in the waist and sleeves, but besides that, it's a perfect fit. I let out the breath I've been holding all week.

"Can I look in the mirror?" she asks, her eyes darting around the empty classroom where I cornered her.

"No. Not until tomorrow," I say.

Then I stick in a few pins and zip the dress into a garment bag before dashing off to Dolce for my second coffee-date-slash-dating-extra-help-session with Kiara.

Kiara is there by the time I arrive, a stuffed tote by her side.

"Those the headpieces?" I ask.

"Yup, all fifteen of them."

I pull a few out and marvel at their beauty. "Thank you," I say. "These are gorgeous. You must've been up all night finishing!"

Kiara shrugs. "I probably would've been anyway."

"Your dad. He got the job?"

She sighs. "Not yet. But he didn't get the one here."

"Oh Kiara." My arms reach for hers as my eyes fill with tears. "I'm so, so sorry."

"Thanks," she says, between sobs. "I wanted to tell you sooner, but I felt like if I talked about it at school, I might start crying and not stop."

I nod, familiar with the feeling.

"Is there anything I can do to help?" I ask.

"Yeah, actually. Tell me tomorrow if the girls like my headpieces. And then practice your heart out for this play. I have tickets to opening night, and it seriously is the only thing I'm looking forward to right now."

I smile. "Well, okay. That I can do. Just as long as you promise me this one thing."

"Yeah?"

"That wherever you end up, there's room for me to visit."

"Really?" she asks.

"Really," I say. And in that moment, I know I've forgiven Kiara. Even though she hurt me, the roots of our friendship never died. All those sleepovers and stories and hours spent at Dolce have led us to where we are today, back in our favorite place. And even though we're each different than we were when we parted ways last fall, it's this history that has brought us back together. That's allowed me to see how much Kiara's changed for the better—how much more sensitive and thoughtful she is. And that's allowed me to see the change in myself. No longer am I the quiet girl shuffling through the halls. Today I have new friends, and a voice—one that's stronger than I could have ever imagined.

Kiara wipes her eyes and leans in for another hug. And when we say goodbye an hour later after picking up the rest of the costumes from Ms. Chloe's, I'm the one who grabs her hand and shakes it.

The next day I awaken feeling lighter than I have in weeks. In fact, forgiving Kiara has made me so relaxed that it's not until halfway through the day when I remember that today is the day: The costume unveiling with Miss Tabitha.

Ava finds me in the hall before my meeting, and we walk over to the high school together. We find Miss Tabitha already there, starting to look at the costumes and headpieces I dropped off with Mom late yesterday afternoon.

"I can't believe how much you've done," she says when we walk in.

"Ms. Chloe did most of it," I say, wondering how I'll ever thank her.

Miss Tabitha flashes Ava and me a quick smile, then pulls out each costume one by one.

"These look amazing! I still can't believe you did this all in a week," she says, then returns to the rack. "And who made this?"

I look up and see her thumbing Cinderella's gown.

"That one's mine," I say, my voice a whisper.

"No way. You really made this?"

I nod.

"You didn't order it? Throw some beads on a prom dress?"

"Nope. It's my own design," I say.

"I'm blown away," she says as she holds the dress up to herself and sways, letting the gentle layers of tulle and chiffon sway back and forth. "It's like a dream. So light and airy. It looks magical!"

"Thanks," I say, grinning. "So are they good enough?" I ask.

"Enough for what?"

"To, you know, use in the play?"

Miss Tabitha laughs. "Oh my goodness, are you kidding me? These may be better than the originals!"

A smile splits my face, and my heart is so full. Ava grabs my hand and we jump up and down, collapsing minutes later into a hug.

"Thank you so much, Jasmine!" says Ava, her hands still locked with mine.

Miss Tabitha nods in agreement. "These costumes will really bring the show to a new level. Thank you for making these happen—you are a real hero!"

"I don't know about that . . ." I say, pinching myself. It's been a long week and the lack of sleep and hours of focus have left my head spinning. But this scene is real. My heart soars as I think about how my gown, the first dress I've made that hasn't been a complete disaster, will soon be paraded around in front of hundreds. I'm helping make Cinderella actually look like Cinderella!

Plus, it's an amazing start to a portfolio for design school—which is originally what I wanted to put together over the winter, before my falling out with Kiara.

"Next year, I'm putting you in charge of costumes from the start!" Miss Tabitha says, eyes dancing. "Maybe we can convince Ms. Chloe to get the whole DIY club involved. We can even see if she'd be interested in running it here at the middle school as an elective."

"Wow, that's a great idea!" I say. I imagine Ms. Chloe's dwindling club filled with new girls eager to learn about fashion design, a room full of machines buzzing with excitement. I think of the backstage closet and envision it filled with Jasmine originals, of creating my own tag to sew in them, of using the costumes as the start of my own clothing line.

Miss Tabitha smiles. "Wonderful. Because something tells me next year you're gonna need some more help. If you keep doing as well as you did in rehearsal today, you're going to have a much bigger part on your hands."

"Really?" I say. I think of this afternoon's practice,

how I ran through my song like I do when singing to the radio alone in my room. How I hit the high notes and held the long ones for emphasis. Afterward, Ana and Samira had cheered for me, and it had felt good. But I still hadn't expected Miss Tabitha to notice. Because as good as my voice sounds in my head, I know it isn't as strong as Ava's. And my range is much smaller than Courtney's. Not to mention they both have me beat in the acting department. But still. *Today is a win*, I think, letting my slightly crooked teeth shine.

"Thank you," I say again. Then Ava and I wave goodbye to Miss Tabitha and spill out onto the street, both of us ready to meet Kiara at Dolce. Thinking of Kiara and her conversation tips, a memory from earlier today comes flooding back. Of Joseph at my locker. I try to hide my grin as I replay our conversation, but find I can't. So I let myself smile wide. And find myself humming under my breath as I wait to tell Ava and Kiara all about it.

"I can't believe you did it!" Ava says, skipping down the sidewalk. "And ohmiGod I can't wait to wear that gown! It's freaking amazing. Like better than a prom dress!"

"Don't get too excited yet," I say, giggling. "You still need one more fitting so I can get it just right."

"Yeah, yeah, whatever. It already looks awesome!" Then Ava stops and pauses, shooting me a sideways glance. "As do you, girl. You're positively glowing."

"What can I say? It's been a very good day," I say.

Ava raises her brow. "Okay. What's up?" she asks.

"What do you mean? You heard Miss Tabitha. We're using our costumes, and I had a good rehearsal. What makes you think there's something more?"

"Because you're giggling! The Jasmine I know laughs and smiles, but is not exactly a giggler."

I shake my head, amazed at how much Ava has gotten to know me.

"All right, well maybe you are on to something."

"Like?"

"Joseph." His name rolls off my lips in a whisper, like a tuft of cotton candy caught in the breeze.

"OhmiGod, what happened? Come on! The suspense is killing me!"

"Five more minutes," I say. "When we get to Dolce. We have to wait for Kiara."

A minute later we push open those familiar glass doors, the smell of ground coffee beans and chocolate surrounding us. Then we skip the line and head straight for Kiara's table. Before we even sit down, I blurt it out.

"Today before rehearsal. He waited for me. At my locker."

"Joseph?" asks Kiara.

"Joseph," I say. "He said we should do something."

"Do something?" says Ava.

I nod. "Uh-huh. Like . . . like a date!"

Chapter Nineteen
IT'S SHOW TIME!

Ava paces around backstage as the stage crew buzzes around us, moving the scenery for the first scene into place.

"So what do you think?" she asks. "Should I put a few more chalk smudges on my cheeks?"

"No, you have enough," I say. "You look perfect."

"For a maid," she says, running her hands through her braids. She's kept them down for this scene, with those in front dangling loose in her face. The longer ones are caught in a rubber band secured at the nape of her neck. And even though she keeps feeling for her bun, I find that she looks even prettier with her braids framing her face—flowing and free. It's how

I think of Ava these days, with her big open heart, never judging and always looking to add another friend to the fold.

"You look gorgeous," I say. "The perfect Cinderella."

"Yes, come here, stepdaughter. I have some more chores for you," says Courtney, sauntering over in her red gown. "You need to wash the carpet, dust the table, polish the silver . . ." She giggles.

"All right, team. Ten minutes to show time. Everyone in scene one, take your places!" says Miss Tabitha, her voice carrying over the whir of the crowd.

My nose itches from the thick yellow face-paint globbed on to look like a beak. I purse my lips together and blow upward, but the breeze does little to stop the tickling. So instead I bring my nail to the tip of my nose, pressing down until I feel relief.

Joseph catches me in the act, surprising me from behind. "Ready, dove?" he asks.

I jump, then nod. "Makeup still okay?"

"Looks good to me."

"Thanks, your highness," I say, curtsying as he adjusts his crown. "You ready too?"

"Can't wait," he says.

My knees shake as I take my place backstage and

wait for my first scene. Even with the shining lights, I know the auditorium is packed. I close my eyes, thinking about everyone who will be watching. Mom, Dad, Abuela, Edwin, and Michael all have front row seats. Lori and Cameron bought tickets last week. Kiara's here with Beatrice and some younger girls from the basketball team. Ms. Chloe said she wouldn't miss it for the world. So many people. So many eyes. As I pace around, my excitement mingles with my nerves.

Ava is on stage now, along with Courtney and the stepsisters. Joseph and Henry are off to the side. They'll be going on soon. And as I look around at my new friends, many in costumes we made ourselves, I can't help but be in awe of all that's happened and all that's yet to come. Like tomorrow's date.

My heart flutters as I picture it. Tomorrow night, after our afternoon performance, Joseph and I will be going to the girls' basketball game. Together. It's the last home game of the season, complete with a bake sale and the school band in attendance, meaning it'll be extra special. My stomach flips at the thought.

Thank goodness for Kiara's conversation tips, I think, then wonder what I'm going to do without her next year. At least her parents decided not to move until school ends in June. But still. We've just made up, and soon she'll be gone.

I try not to dwell on this as the music picks up and Ava's strong, clear voice bounces off the walls backstage. We're in the second scene now, about ten minutes into the play. I've got about fifteen more minutes until Miss Tabitha lines me up. I walk over to the refreshments table, grab a bottle of water, and sip slowly through a purple straw.

Ava is offstage now, and from afar I see her jumping, her whole body a ball of energy, just like it was the first time I saw her perform. She's killing it! Judging by Miss Tabitha's smile as she darts back and forth like a gnat, sending kids on and off stage, I'm sure she thinks so too. I hear Joseph and Henry onstage. King and prince. Again, I think of tomorrow and my whole face warms.

"You ready?" asks Courtney, joining me backstage.

"Yeah, how's it going out there?"

"So far, so good," she says. "The audience seems really into it."

"I heard you singing before. Everyone sounds fantastic!"

"Thanks," she says before running back toward the stage, her long dress dusting the floor beneath it.

A moment later I'm face to face with Miss Tabitha, who's leading me to the side.

"You're on in five," she says, leaving me in the shadows. When the lights dim, I waltz out with Ana and Samira and take my place next to Ava.

And then it's time for the song with my solo. The song starts slow and sweet, and I hit the notes with ease. I do as Ava told me, being sure to look up when I look out, and to think only of Cinderella and the fairy godmother and the play. I sing and flit around the stage as if I really am a dove. As if Joseph wasn't watching from the sidelines. As if everyone I know wasn't in the audience.

Instead, I breathe in and sing, the notes coming out stronger and clearer as I build momentum. As I enter the last verse, the nerves in my stomach buzz, their memory of that last high note strong. It's a little out of my range, and I've fallen short just as many times as I've gotten it right. But tonight is one of the lucky ones. The note comes out loud and clear and on key. I fight the urge to cheer as the piano hits the last note. And then, before I can even think about what just happened, the lights are dimming once again. So I glide off the stage toward Miss Tabitha's fluttering hands, Courtney's big thumbs-up, and Joseph's wide smile.

"You were amazing," he says as I walk by, Miss Tabitha already ushering me backstage.

"Good luck," I mouth to him, knowing it's almost time for his big scene.

And then I find myself jumping just like Ava was minutes earlier. The energy continues as I run on and off the stage, singing with the animals again and then with the chorus, until I'm sandwiched between Ana and Samira, taking my final bow. The audience is roaring, everyone on their feet. They scream the loudest for Ava and Henry, who run out last, holding hands and smiling so wide I wonder if their cheeks hurt. But I realize I'm smiling just as wide. Then the curtain closes and Ava and Henry drop their grins to let out a roar of their own.

"We did it!" they say and we all scream back.

The stage is charged with the energy of a successful opening night, and I wonder how we will ever repeat this magic for the rest of the performances. But Ava says we will, and as I see her hugging Miss Tabitha, her eyes bright with excitement, I know she's right.

After hugging Ava and Courtney, I run out into the school lobby, eager to find my family. The crowd is thick, filled with parents and friends and relatives, all smiling and patting backs, congratulating the cast on a job well done. Lori and Cameron find me first. They pull me into a hug before offering their congratulations.

"You were excellent! Tonight was so fun!" says Lori with a wave.

"Thanks," I say, then continue my search for my family.

I spot Michael on Dad's shoulders.

"Hey! Over here," I say, waving my hands. But I'm short and the crowd's busy, so I give up on getting his attention and run toward them instead.

"Here's the star!" Dad says when they spot me, and before I know it, I'm surrounded by their squeals and shouts. They shower me in flowers and praise and make me feel so warm and loved and proud. As I walk out of the building and into the crisp night with my family surrounding me, all I can think about is how happy and proud and energized I am right now in this moment.

Chapter Twenty
PLUM PERFECT

I stand in front of my closet and squint, letting the slivers of purples and blues and pinks all swirl together like a marble, hoping that if I stand here long enough, something will leap out and tell me to wear it. But as my eyes start to cross like they do when I try to do one of those hidden pictures—to this day I've never seen anything but dots—I decide just to go with the outfit Kiara suggested last week. The new pink striped sweater Mom got me for Christmas, and my favorite faded jeans. Above my door, the old-fashioned cuckoo clock Abuela gave me for my fifth birthday springs to life. It's four o'clock. The game starts at five. Usually that would mean I'd have a half hour to throw on some clothes and bolt out the door, but tonight is different. Because tonight I'm catching a ride.

I was a little nervous when Joseph said he'd pick me up—the thought of having to talk to his parents is more than a little scary—but Ava was there when he asked and she agreed for me before I could say no. According to her, getting picked up is an important part of a date. Given that all either one of us knows about dates is what we've seen on television, I'm not exactly sure I agree with her assessment. Especially after conferring with Kiara, who claimed that when she went to the movies with Carter he met her there. But by the time I could tell this to Ava, the damage was done, and Joseph's dad was planning on stopping by our house ten minutes before game time. At that point, I was more nervous of what Joseph would think if I said I'd just meet him instead, so I decided to let our plans stand. But the anticipation of that three-minute ride haunts me as I pull on my jeans and sweater.

Thank goodness I live close to the school, I think, getting to work on my hair. It's a half-dried mess of curls and for a minute I'm tempted just to grab one of the headbands Kiara made for me and throw it over a ponytail. But then I think of how let down Ava and Kiara and Courtney will be if they see me not sticking to our plan, so I reach for the blow-dryer and styling cream Kiara gave me. It takes thirty minutes to dry my hair, but in the end it's worth it. My hair ends up not exactly straight, but not curly either. Instead, it's something in the middle, and I can't help but smile as I inspect the shiny black waves framing my face.

Satisfied, I run downstairs to the kitchen for a snack. I bite into a granola bar just as Mom enters the front door with the twins, their arms heavy with groceries.

"Oh good, you're still here," she says, giving me a kiss on my cheek. "I was hoping we wouldn't miss you."

"Nope. He should be here soon, though."

Mom turns to the clock on her phone and nods. She's met Joseph a few times now, during rehearsals and then after the play, but I can tell that she still wanted to be here for the big pickup for my first real date. She puts down the groceries, then turns to me and smiles.

"You look so beautiful," she says. "Here. I got you something to take with you."

She fumbles with a bag, then hands me a lip gloss.

"Plum perfect," I say, reading the wrapper. It's the first time Mom's ever gotten me anything but clear gloss and for a moment I'm nervous to put it on. But as Mom waves me over to the bathroom, I relax.

"Go on, give it a try," she says. "If you don't like it, you can take it off. But it should bring out the gold flecks in your eyes."

I smile, then give the tube a squeeze and rub a drop over my lips. And I see that Mom's right. My eyes do look brighter.

"I know you don't need any makeup to look beautiful, but I couldn't resist," she says. "I think I was about your age when I started wearing colored gloss. Figured maybe it was time for you to try it too."

My cheeks burn as I throw the purple tube into the bag Mary Beth once laughed at, and start pacing back and forth. Mom eyes my bag and nods, and I can tell she's as happy as I am that I've decided to keep using it.

"So when does the JKDesigns site go live?" she asks, trying to keep her eyes off the clock.

"The weekend after next," I say. "After the play and basketball end."

"That's great. I'm so glad you're still doing it," Mom says.

I nod, thinking back to the day last week when Kiara asked if I still had my bags.

"Me too. And it really is the perfect way for Kiara and me to stay in touch. With the store, we'll still have something we can do together, even though we're hundreds of miles apart."

"I'm so happy you girls worked things out."

"I just wish she wasn't moving away."

"I know, though judging by what you two endured this year, I think it's safe to say you're destined to be friends for the long haul."

"Yeah, I think so too. And who knows? Maybe one day we'll end up together in college. Preferably one focused on design."

"Or theater," Mom says with a wink.

"Or science," I say, surprising myself. "Ms. Cabot says I have one of the highest grades in the class."

"Well, any of those things would be wonderful. Just as long as it's something you love."

My heart skips a beat as I hear the familiar thud of footsteps outside.

"That must be him," I say, as he rings the bell.

"Wait here," Mom says, running to the door. She opens it wide and greets Joseph with a handshake.

He steps in and right away I'm glad I did my hair. Because gone is his faded Yankees cap and typical tattered T-shirt. Instead, his hair is neatly combed, a green polo falling over a slim pair of jeans.

"You look nice," he says, and I realize that all the time I've been staring at him, he's been staring at me.

I open my mouth to say the same, but find my throat too dry to speak. So instead I look back at Mom who, sensing my nerves, breaks the silence with a quick hug and a wave.

"Have fun tonight," she says, nudging me toward the door. "And tell Kiara good luck! I know she's going to do great!"

"Thanks Mom," I say, finding my voice, then follow Joseph to the car where he already has the passenger door open and waiting.

I breathe in deep and duck inside, greeting his dad as I secure my seatbelt. And by the time I'm buckled and he's done saying hello, the school is in sight. The ride I've been stressing about all week is over.

"Thanks Mr. Cruz," I say, as Joseph opens my door and waits for me to exit.

"No problem. Have fun, kids," he says. "I'll be right here to grab you around seven. Call me if anything changes!"

"Oh, actually Dad, do you think you can make it 7:30? In front of Dolce?" Joseph asks. "Your parents would be cool with that, right? Getting home a little later? I thought maybe we could go, you know, grab a drink. And maybe if anyone else is around, we can see if they want to go too . . ."

I nod as Joseph fumbles over the words, his eyes darting from side to side. I can tell he's nervous, and it makes him even more adorable than usual.

"Yeah sure, I'll just shoot them a text. But 7:30 should be fine."

Joseph exhales, then smiles, his face softening.

"All right then. Seven thirty at Dolce it is," says Mr. Cruz before pulling away.

Then as we face the school, ready for the same walk inside that we make every day, Joseph grabs my hand. And all of a sudden, everything around me is brand new. The rock salt scattered on the concrete walkway, the dim orange lights shining down from the metal awning. They sparkle in the setting sun, transporting me far away from the troubles of middle school to somewhere alive and magical and beautiful, like a dream. *So this is what it feels like to like a boy*, I think, taking a deep breath of cool March air.

As we walk, Joseph threads his fingers through mine, then flashes me the same bright smile that first made my heart flip when he was the mystery boy I saw shuffling down the hall.

"You okay?" he asks as we reach the door, his arm already outstretched and ready to open it for me.

"Yeah, I'm great," I say.

"Me too," he says. "Never better."

I laugh as we pass by the bake sale, my stomach flip-flopping when I think of the conversation I'll have about this later tonight with Kiara and Ava. My mind wanders, and so does my gaze, until it stops on a stack of papers at the end of the table. I reach out my free hand and grab one.

"What's that?" asks Joseph, leaning over.

"Looks like the new Parks and Rec flyer," I say. "For summer."

"Cool. Wonder if there's anything good."

I shrug. "I dunno, but I thought I'd see if there was a singing class. Miss Tabitha was saying it might be a good idea to keep practicing."

Joseph smiles wider. "That would be great! Your voice is amazing. Can you imagine how good you'd be after a real singing class? You'd be good enough for one of those TV shows!"

"Well, I don't know about that, but it could be fun to try something new," I say. The words roll off my tongue before I can think about them, though after I do, I find that I mean them.

"You should definitely do it. It'll get you ready for Fall Theater," Joseph says.

"Yes! And it'd be a good release from all that sewing Kiara and I have planned for JKDesigns."

"Sounds like the perfect fit," he says, squeezing my hand a little tighter as we reach the entrance to the gym.

As I think of Ava and Kiara and Courtney waiting for me inside, I can't help but think of that day a couple months earlier when Mom made me try that first drama class. Imagining that first meeting, I have to laugh. Back then I never could've pictured my friendship with Ava or Joseph, or even my reunion with Kiara and return to fashion design. All I could think about was how to survive that day and tell Mom I was quitting. But then I ran into Ava at school and I kept going to practices and found that acting wasn't as scary as I thought.

And that's when it hits me. How happy I am now. How drama has changed me. And I realize that maybe sometimes in order to find what you love and discover what really makes you happy, you need to forge a new path. It might take you somewhere new, or it might bring you right back to where you started—but when you return, you'll never be exactly the same. Like today. Here I am back at the school gym, ready to watch Kiara. Only today I'm so much stronger than I was during that first game. And my life has become so much fuller—from drama club, and new friends, and Joseph, and learning to forgive Kiara.

We're in the gym now, staring up into the bleachers. My eyes scan the crowd, looking for Ava, Courtney, and Henry. They're up there toward the top, waving. Joseph waves his free hand back, then leads me up the bleachers to where they've saved a spot. We take our time, letting both feet hit each bleacher before tackling the next. And as we make the climb, I hold my head high and smile out at the crowd, which I know is already buzzing with the news of us holding hands. When we reach Ava, we both move to sit down and, for a moment, our knees touch. A bolt of electricity shoots down my leg and I smile, enjoying the new sensation. Then I look over at Courtney, who's joking with Henry, their hands also touching. Ava rolls her eyes and Joseph laughs and I laugh with him as the first buzzer rings. Then I sit back and clap as our team charges the court, excited for whatever may lie ahead.

SWIRL

Pumpkin Spice Secrets
by Hillary Homzie

Sometimes secrets aren't so sweet . . .

When Maddie spills her pumpkin spice drink on a
cute boy, she's instantly smitten. But add best friend
drama and major school stress to Maddie's secret
coffee shop crush, and it's a recipe for disaster. Can
she stay true to both her friend and her heart?

Sky Pony Press
New York

Peppermint Cocoa Crushes

by Laney Nielson

Friends, cocoa, crushes…catastrophe!

'Tis the season for snow, gifts, peppermint cocoa, and the school's variety show competition! But Sasha's head is spinning between rehearsals, homework, and volunteer commitments. Can she make the most of her moment in the spotlight?

Sky Pony Press
New York

Cinnamon Bun Besties

by Stacia Deutsch

It's bestie vs. bestie . . .

When the Valentine's Day fundraiser Suki is running gets out of control and the local animal shelter where she volunteers is in danger of closing, she's determined to save the day. But she can't do it alone—and her only hope for help is her worst enemy . . .

Sky Pony Press
New York

ABOUT THE AUTHOR

Jackie Nastri Bardenwerper is the author of young adult novels *On the Line* and *Populatti*. She loves fishing, running, and the beach. She graduated from Cornell University and lives in Fairfield, Connecticut with her husband and two children. Visit her online at www.jnbwrite.com.